Verbal Ecstasy

Erotic Short Stories
of The Digital Age

S. RIZVI

Copyright © 2019 S. Rizvi

All rights reserved. No part of this publication may be reproduced, distributed, or transmitted in any form or by any means, including photocopying, recording, or other electronic or mechanical methods, without the prior written permission of the publisher, except in the case of brief quotations embodied in critical reviews and certain other noncommercial uses permitted by copyright law. For permission requests, email the publisher, with subject: "Verbal Ecstasy Copyright Permissions" at the email address below.

ISBN: 978-0-578-54913-2

This is a work of fiction. Names, characters, businesses, places, events, locales, and incidents are either the products of the author's imagination or used in a fictitious manner. Any resemblance to actual persons, living or dead, or actual events is purely coincidental.

Cover design by S. Rizvi

First printing edition 2019

S. Rizvi
me@verbalecstasy.com

www.verbalecstasy.com

DEDICATION

I dedicate this book to all the women of the world. You are the representation of love, creation, beauty, strength, compassion, nurture and sexuality. Without you, life would not exist. You are to be respected and loved to the utmost for the service you provide to humanity and its existence.

CONTENTS

1 Tinder Squad 1

2 MILF on Fleek 13

3 YOLO Target 21

4 Savage Boss 26

5 Uber Thirst Trap 33

6 Airplane AF 38

7 Duck Face Riders 45

8 Police Finesse 51

9 Lit Train 56

10 Turnt Beach 62

11 Drive-thru Crunk 67

12 Straight Fire Delivery 76

13 Gucci Gift 85

14 Subway Ratchet 93

15 Yacht Zaddy 100

1 TINDER SQUAD

Molly is sitting in her balcony enjoying a nice hot cup of green tea while gazing at the Santa Monica beach shoreline in the bright Sunday morning sun. With her cup in one hand she is holding her phone and swiping left on every guy she sees on Tinder. She has been on this app for a few months and so far it has been pretty disappointing for her. Every time she sees a guy she likes, the moment she scrolls right to see his other pictures, she is turned off by either a topless selfie in a dirty bathroom mirror, a picture proudly showing off assault rifles in the boonies with empty crushed beer cans in the background, or more than one picture of the guy playing with his cats, yes cats and not *a* cat. One of her biggest turn-offs is a guy in love with his cat, let alone multiple cats. She doesn't quite know why but it bothers her. Maybe one day she will figure out exactly why.

Swiping away on her phone, she comes across an Italian guy. Now she's had her fair share of Italian stallions in her life, but this guy looks and seems different. He's definitely not young. He is what you might call a daddy in today's day and age. He is in his mid to late forties with some grey hair around the temples. He's got a little stubble going in some of his pics which is a big turn-on for her. Not everyone in her opinion can pull off a stubble, but in his case, he's got just the right amount of facial hair going which accentuates his chiseled, tan, Italian modelesque features. He has broad shoulders and seems to be pretty tall. He kind of reminds her of a nineties Ridge Forrester from The Bold and the Beautiful soap opera. He was her childhood celebrity crush. Oh the dirty dreams she's had of him growing up. She has to snap back into present time as she notices herself drift away into her day dreams. She's been doing that quite often lately with her sexual drought going strong into the third month. She really needs to get her plumbing cleaned soon before she ends up turning into a nun.

She likes his name too – Lorenzo. She can feel a tingling sensation in her vagina. She quickly swipes right on his picture and decides to go take a shower. She might have to pleasure herself in the shower, she thinks. It might be the only sex she will be getting today considering the weekend is almost over. She just got her nails done and got a fresh natural tan at the beach which she feels is going to waste. Oh well…just another day in the life of a single, successful early-thirties' woman living the life of her prime in the City of Angels.

She loves this new shower head she bought from Amazon recently. It is very multifunctional in that it has a great waterfall setting which has just the right amount of water pressure, giving the beads of water just the right amount of size and volume so that the water massages your body without stinging you. Another great feature is that when she turns the dial on the shower head in just the right direction, the water comes out in a pulsating vibrating motion – the kind of water that when she directs over to her vaginal area gives her the feeling of immense pleasure to the extent of orgasm. She never knew she could cum with water pressure. You live and learn.

She assumes the position with one leg up on the edge

of the bathtub while she opens her legs up so her inner thighs are facing front and goes to town with the showerhead. The pulsating vibrating steady stream of warm water hits her clit and pussy lips and she immediately closes her eyes. It's great that she doesn't even have to touch her pussy and she can cum. It's revolutionary in her opinion. Ah the simple technological pleasures of the 21st century! She feels the warm sensation of an incoming orgasm take over her body and she starts to shake a little, her legs quivering, as she moans and cums at the same time. The rest of the shower is like a fairy tale for her.

She comes out, dries herself and checks her phone. Lorenzo has not matched with her.

"Well obviously Lorenzo is a married man who is probably spending time with his wife and kids on this beautiful Sunday," she imagines. "He must be a cheater that asshole."

She quickly realizes her irrational thought pattern and forces herself to think of something less neurotic. She smiles as she thinks about going to the local grocery store to buy her favorite bottle of merlot. She plans to spend the rest of the evening watching her favorite shows on Netflix with a couple glasses of wine and then fall asleep alone for the work day tomorrow. But what she is really smiling about is the fact that Saeed, the cashier at the grocery store, is working today and she will get to flirt with him.

"Oh my God! I'm such a creep for knowing Saeed's work schedule," she thinks and laughs to herself.

She finds her favorite wine and looks at the lines at all the cash registers. Even though, the register Saeed is working at has the longest line, she decides to wait. Her desperation is sad and makes herself chuckle. She may be desperate for attention but she is also pretty sexy and confident in herself and her abilities. Everyone has dry seasons and it just so happens to be hers right now.

"Hi Saeed! How are you doing today? Busy day?" she asks as her turn arrives at the cash register.

"Oh hi Molly! Well you know how it is on Sundays, just peachy!" he replies.

They both laugh in unison.

"Any big plans for tonight?" she asks with a big grin on her face.

"Not really. Not yet anyway. But I know you will be spending the night with this handsome bottle aren't you?" he points at the merlot.

"Oh you know me Saeed…the wild child. Even my name stands for a popular party drug!" she laughs. "Hey, speaking of which, you said you have the hook up to some really good molly?"

"Yeah I'll have to check with my buddy first before I give out his number. But if you give me yours, I'll text you later tonight."

"Yeah sure! You wanna feed it to me…shit…I mean feed your number in my phone?" She feels so stupid. She is totally giving him open signals to put his big middle-eastern cock in her mouth.

"Hahaha…oookay then!" He puts his number in her phone.

She quickly texts him so he has her number too. "Ok talk to you later Saeed!"

She curses herself as she walks to her car. But she's kind of not sorry. She's been wanting to go out with Saeed for the longest time. He is a tall, dark and handsome young middle-eastern man. And she knows he's got a big cock from the size of his hands and feet and his slightly bigger than average nose. The two middle-eastern men she has slept with both had pretty huge dicks. She really hopes to get a text from him tonight, even if it is to say he couldn't get in touch with his friend. In fact, she doesn't even do any drugs. She just wants to badly be fucked by him over her kitchen countertop while she bends over and he fucks her from behind while pulling on her hair and kissing her neck.

As she sits in her car, her phone buzzes. She looks at it

and is happy to see that Lorenzo has finally matched with her. "Yesss you horny little bitch! Your Italian stallion wants to fuck the shit of you," she mumbles as she drives back to her place.

She opens the app as soon as she gets home and Lorenzo has messaged her already. She waits a good thirty minutes to reply back as to not seem desperate – just the protocol of online dating. She replies back and tells him she's just relaxing at home with some merlot. He replies back saying he'd love to meet up for a drink. She thinks about it a little before she opens her bottle of wine and decides to reply back to him telling him to meet at the bar downstairs of her fancy condominium building.

She doesn't really take Tinder that seriously and hence makes these spontaneous plans, most of which don't even come through. Either she flakes out or the guy. She doesn't think Lorenzo will come through either. So she doesn't even bother changing and sips on a glass of wine while watching a show on Netflix.

"I'm here," she reads a message from Lorenzo.

"Oh shit shit shit! I haven't even dressed up," she shouts. She quickly changes into her go-to SBD (short black dress) and brushes her hair into an Ariana Grande style high ponytail. You cannot go wrong with the look. She doesn't need a lot of makeup as she has naturally good skin. She just puts on a little foundation and lipstick, wears her favorite Christian Louboutin pumps and is ready to seduce Lorenzo.

She walks into the bar and sees him sitting at the front. They both look at each other with lustful gazes and are very touchy feely right off the bat. She really wants to fuck him tonight and what better bar to meet at than the one directly below her condo. If this guy doesn't turn out to be a total douchebag, she might just fuck his brains out tonight.

She excuses herself to go to the bathroom and while she is fixing herself up in front of the mirror, she gets a text. She looks at her phone and it's Saeed.

"Hey Molly. So bad news is that I couldn't get in touch with the guy but I do have some badass weed if you want some," he writes.

"Oh fuck yes I do," she replies. "I'm actually having a drink at the bar downstairs of my condo building…you wanna come meet me here?"

"Yeah sure. Let me google it. Ok it's only 7 minutes away. Ok so see you there in a bit."

"Yes see you soon Saeed."

She knows exactly what she's doing. It has always been her fantasy to fuck two exotic guys at the same time. She is staging an exotic threesome. She has to be careful though. Not all men are willing to do something like that as they tend to get very territorial. But if the guys are as open-minded as she thinks they are, it might just happen.

"Two cocks are better than one for sure," she thinks.

She walks out to the bar and asks Lorenzo if he smokes weed. He responds in the affirmative. Then she goes on to tell him that her weed dealer might be dropping by to give her some weed and if that's ok with him. He doesn't mind at all.

Saeed arrives at the right time when Molly and Lorenzo are quite tipsy. He doesn't know what to expect so he just walks up to Molly and says, "Hey you! You look amazing!"

"Oh hey Saeed! Thank you! You look and smell great!" They hug. "Oh I want you to meet Lorenzo. Lorenzo this is Saeed my friend. Saeed this is Lorenzo, my Tinder date."

The men greet each other with straight faces as though the alpha males have just crossed each other's territories.

Molly senses the tension and quickly tries to dissipate it. "Hey guys. So how do I look?" She stands up and turns around to show off her round perky ass. "I've been working out for the last 2 months on my ass. How does it look you guys?"

The two men turn their heads quick like ninjas to stare at her ass.

"Yeah yeah it looks amazing," Lorenzo replies.

"Oh but I already know how good your ass looks Molly. I see you every week," Saeed replies in a competitive tone.

"Ok I really wanna smoke some weed guys. Let's go up to my condo. Shall we?" she beams.

She guides them to the elevator up to her condo. She has an amazing apartment. It is very chic and modern. She has a big white leather L-shaped couch in her living room where she invites the men to come sit. Saeed quickly gets down to rolling a joint. He offers it to her to light it up. She takes a long puff and passes it back to Saeed.

"This is good weed Saeed!" she exclaims.

"I only smoke the best," he quickly replies. "Here bro, have some."

"Nah I'm ok guys. I don't smoke that much," Lorenzo replies.

"Oh that's ok sweetie. You want some merlot?" she asks him.

"Yes that would be great thanks," he answers.

She gets him a glass and the merlot bottle. Everyone is feeling pretty damn good at this point. She decides to make the first move by showing off the shape and size of her ass that she's so proud off by getting down on her hands and knees and pretending to look for the remote under her couch.

"Guys I can't find my remote," she says while arching her back and sticking her ass up in the air. Her dress lifts up from her thighs to the point where it shows off the bottom curves of her ass cheeks.

The guys look at each other and smile with a sense of camaraderie. Saeed decides to make a bold move. He reaches out and gently smacks her ass.

"Oh shit Saeed! You naughty boy! You like that ass don't you?" she asks.

"It is a great ass. Sorry I couldn't help. It was so instinctive," he replies.

"Oh don't be sorry babe. I liked it."

"Then come here…" He lifts her up and places her right on top of his lap.

"Oh my God! You're already so hard," she says while grabbing his crotch.

They start kissing passionately. She has waited so long for this moment. She used to fantasize kissing Saeed's perfect lips and caressing his jawline as she kisses his mouth and look into his dark brown exotic eyes. It's finally coming to fruition. She just didn't realize it would be in such a circumstance. They both kiss and suck on each other's lips while their hands explore each other's bodies, grabbing, rubbing and squeezing as they make out passionately.

Saeed is quick in undressing her. He simply grabs on to her dress from the bottom and pulls it from over her head while she lifts her hands straight up in the air. He buries his face in her tits and sniffs her perfume as he reaches with his left index finger and thumb to smoothly unhook her bra.

"Wow you've got some moves Saeed!" she exclaims.

All this while, Lorenzo sips on his wine and just watches, waiting for the right time to join in the fun.

Saeed grabs and squeezes her tits and flicks her erect nipples with the tip of his tongue, alternating between the two and then puts one of them in his soft, warm and wet mouth, sucking and gently nibbling on them. She squirms and moans with pleasure. She can take it a little rough and he has just found out. So he tries to test her limits. He grabs her ponytail and pulls on it a little while nibbling on her nipple and she moans louder. He likes the fact that she likes it a little rough because he loves to give it rough to girls who can handle it. He slaps one of her tits and she looks straight into his eyes and smiles as if beckoning for rougher treatment. He gets even harder. He lifts her up and puts her on the ground and stands up in front of her. He holds her head and pushes her face in his crotch. She growls and gently bites on his erection over his boxers. She grabs the elastic of his boxers in her teeth and pulls them off, revealing his big, thick, long and hard cock.

"Oh fuck! You're so big!" she exclaims.

He smiles and holds his cock from the shaft and shoves it in her mouth. He holds her head and starts pumping and thrusting his hard cock deeper down her throat until she gags on it. She pulls out the cock from her mouth and licks on his balls. Her saliva drips from the sides of her mouth as she sucks on his big juicy balls. He grabs his hard erect throbbing cock and slaps her cheeks with it. She loves it. He rubs his cock all over her face then pushes it back in her mouth, even deeper until her lips touch his balls. She can take it all in like a champ. He then lifts her up and throws her on the couch, spreads open her legs and holds them by her ankles. Her pussy is dripping wet. He kisses her legs from her ankles all the way to her inner thighs. He bites her inner thighs, just inches away from her throbbing wet juicy pussy. She can't wait for him to put his mouth and tongue on her dripping wet pussy. He slowly brings his mouth over her pussy and licks her clit with the tip of his tongue. She throws her head back in ecstasy and moans louder. She places her hand on the back of his head and runs her fingers through his hair as he licks her wet juicy warm pussy and slides his soft warm wet tongue in between her pussy lips, up and down and licking her clit. She is in heaven. He is really good at eating pussy. She starts to cum. Her body starts to shake and quiver.

She screams with ecstasy. "Aaaaahhhhh baby! Fuck yessssss! Oh fuck baby! I'm cumming!"

Lorenzo is rock hard now and wants to join in. He stands up, drops his pants and pulls out his cock. It's not as big as Saeed's but it's above average for sure. He puts his cock in her mouth while Saeed eats her out. It is a full-on threesome now. He pumps his hard cock in her mouth. She closes her eyes and submits herself completely to these two men.

Saeed gets up and rubs his cock head on her wet pussy, taps her pussy lips with his shaft and then shoves it balls deep in her pussy. She gasps as he goes balls deep and starts thrusting and pounding her pussy hard, fast and deep. She moans with a mouthful of cock. It is very kinky and sexually satisfying for her to have one cock in her pussy while one in her mouth. Both men pumping their big hard cocks in her mouth and pussy looks like a scene directly from a porno.

Saeed lifts her up from her waist, sits on the couch and puts her pussy right on top of his cock so she can ride it. She wraps her arms around his neck and bounces up and down, up and down, up and down on his hard throbbing cock which fills her pussy and hits her insides. She has never felt so filled up. Her ass cheeks slap against his thighs and pelvis and the flesh-clapping sound echoes in her room.

Lorenzo finds a perfect opportunity to get behind her and spits on her asshole. She turns around and gives him the look of approval. He rubs his spit on her ass hole and then slowly inserts his cock in her ass. Saeed stops moving so Lorenzo can go slow. He slowly puts half his cock inside her ass and she moans loud with a mixture of pain and pleasure. He then spits on her ass hole again and then pushes his hard cock deeper in her ass until he is fully inserted. She has never felt this sensation before of being double-penetrated. It is mind-blowing for her.

Both the men start thrusting her holes at the same time. She is screaming with pleasure. Lorenzo fucks her ass while Saeed fucks her pussy. It can't get any better than this for her.

Lorenzo takes his cock out and then puts it in her mouth. She sucks on it like it's her first meal in two days. She gobbles it all up while Saeed continues to fuck her pussy. Saeed then lifts her up and puts her on the couch so she can be on all her fours. She arches her back and lifts her ass up for him. He shoves his hard cock doggy style into her juicy pussy and pumps it in and out, in and out, in and out, while grabbing and squeezing both her ass cheeks. He slaps her ass hard and she screams with pleasure and pain. Lorenzo continues to fuck her face deep. Saeed reaches for her tits and squeezes them as he fucks her doggy. Her ass slaps against his pelvis and upper thighs.

The men then switch positions. Saeed holds her head and fucks it deep till she gags on it. He grabs her by her throat and can feel his cock head down her throat as he fucks it deep. He holds on to her hair and pulls on it as she pushes her face deep down his shaft till her lips touch his ball sack.

Lorenzo fucks her deep and fast while slapping her ass. She cums again; it's the fourth time. He then pulls out his cock and puts it in her ass. She squirms. He pulls her hair and starts fucking her ass deep and fast and rough.

Saeed can't take it anymore and gets close to orgasm. Lorenzo also gets closer and closer to cumming. Saeed's moans become louder and he pulls his cock out from her mouth and strokes it. Lorenzo pulls out his cock and she knows the guys are about to cum. She gets down on the floor on her knees and holds both the cocks in her hands. She alternatively sucks on their cocks. Lorenzo starts to moan louder. He strokes his cock vigorously as she sucks on his balls and looks up into his eyes to see the pleasure he is experiencing.

He starts to cum. "Argh! Arrgghh! Aaarrrggghhh!" He shoots his warm cum all over her face while she opens her mouth and sticks her tongue out.

"Yes baby cum all over my face," she shouts.

Lorenzo cums a big load all over her face and open mouth.

Saeed starts to moan louder as well. She then starts sucking on his balls and waits for his cum to shoot all over her face.

He shouts, "Aaahhh fuck! Aaarrrggghhh fuck fuck fuck! Aaarrrggghhh baby take this cum you nasty cum-guzzling slut." He starts to cum on her face.

She takes his cock in her mouth because she wants to swallow the rest of it. He cums a big load in her mouth and she gulps it down. She then squeezes the tip of his cock head to get every single drop of his cum out. She licks the tip of his cock head and licks her lips.

"Yummy cummy," she says.

They all start laughing.

2 MILF ON FLEEK

Nick does the final inventory of his pickup truck. He's got all his equipment ready for the day. He's got eight pools to clean today. He likes Mondays since he goes to Hollywood Hills to clean some really nice pools. It's one of the perks of his job and he loves dreaming about owning such a house in the hills someday. He wants to own his very own pool cleaning company and is trying to save up money for it. That will be his ticket to financial freedom.

It's a nice day with a few clouds in the sky. Nick is driving up the hills and enjoying the view from up here. The day has gone by pretty quickly. He is on his last house of the day. He pulls into the long winding driveway that takes him down to the entrance of this beautiful mansion. This is probably the fifth or sixth time he has worked on this pool and he wonders if anyone even lives here. He has never seen anyone even walk past the kitchen that is clearly visible through the floor-to-ceiling windows that this whole house seems to be built of.

The gate to the pool is always open so he pulls his pool cleaning equipment through. He can't help but admire the beautiful architecture of this house. The morning rays of sunshine flow in dramatically through the scattered clouds into the living room that is furnished with elegant white leather couches. The white marble countertops glisten golden with the sun's rays.

"One day," he whispers as he pulls out his pool skimmer and starts cleaning the Olympic-sized infinity pool that overlooks the hills below.

He is halfway done skimming the pool when he catches a glimpse of the first sign of human life he has seen at this house. He is almost startled and pauses to look who it is. A woman walks over to the kitchen adorned in what seems to be a white silk robe. She turns her head to look at him and he immediately and awkwardly goes back to cleaning the pool. He doesn't want to seem like a peeping tom. A few minutes later, he hears the sliding glass doors open so he turns his head to look.

"Good morning," says the woman.

"Oh hi…good morning to you too Ma'am," he replies.

"Hahaha oh please! I'm very far away from being a Ma'am. Just call me Mandi. What's your name?" the woman says as she walks up to him with a cup of coffee in her hand.

He puts the skimmer on the ground, wipes his hand on his shirt and extends his hand out. "Hi Mandi, I'm Nick…sorry my hands are wet."

"Oh you think I'm afraid to get a little dirty?"

"Oh no I didn't mean it like that."

"It's ok…relax Nick…I'm only pulling your leg."

They both laugh.

She sits on the pool lounger and takes a sip of her coffee while her robe slips to the sides revealing her toned legs. "Can I get you anything?"

"No thank you I'm good. I'm almost done," he replies.

"Are you in a hurry to leave?"

"Not really no"

"Well then take your time Nick. I won't bother you. You do your thing and I'll do mine."

He continues cleaning the pool. He is getting a little

nervous as she keeps looking at him while he works.

"Do you mind me staring at you Nick?"

"Hahaha. Oh I didn't notice you were staring."

"I like to watch men work. I just find it sexy watching you handle your equipment with such mastery."

"It's honestly not that hard or complicated of a job."

"Never undermine what you do for work."

He finishes refilling the chlorine dispenser and loads up his tool trolley.

"Before you leave Nick, can I ask you a huge favor?" she asks.

"Oh sure! How can I be of assistance?" he responds.

"Do you know anything about leaking pipes?"

"Actually I don't."

"Ah that's too bad. Oh well…"

"I can take a look though and at least tell you where it's leaking from so you can call a plumber."

"Would you be a sweetheart and do that please?"

"Sure no problem."

She gets up from her lounger, adjusts the belt of her robe and elegantly escorts him into her kitchen. She opens the kitchen sink cabinet. "It's been bothering me for days."

He kneels down and inspects the pipes. "I honestly can't see any leaks."

"Oh really? Hmm…I guess I must be going senile then."

He stands up and turns around to face her and is startled to see that her robe is parted in the middle, revealing half of her tits. "Oh shit sorry."

"What are you apologizing for? Have you never seen boobs before?" She walks up really close to him. "Listen Nick, let me be completely honest. My husband left work today without fucking me like the cum-guzzling slut that I am and I need you to fix my leaking pipes."

She grabs his hand and places it over her pussy. "Do you feel how fuckin' wet I am?"

One touch of her wet pussy and he immediately starts

getting hard.

She looks at his bulging crotch and starts rubbing it over his shorts. "Damn baby…that is a thick cock! Pull it out and fuck my fuckin' face already!"

He gets rock hard hearing her say that and pulls down his shorts. She gets down on her knees in front of him. He takes his hard cock out and shoves it in her mouth.

"*Gluk…gluk…gluk…*" her throat sounds as he pumps his hard cock in her mouth. She gasps for air. "Fuck my throat harder! Use me Nick! Abuse me! Disrespect me! Make me your fuck toy! Fuck me as rough as you can!"

He holds her head and starts fucking her throat really rough. Her saliva drips out the side of her mouth as he grabs her head and fucks her mouth like it was a pocket pussy. He has had his share of sex in his life but he has never been told by a woman to go as rough as he can. And this utterly dominant position is turning him on like never before. He is going to take full advantage of this situation to fulfill his no-limits rough sex fantasy.

He picks her up by her waist, she wraps her legs around his and they take it to the couch.

"Damn baby, you're strong," she says as she touches his biceps in awe.

He puts her down on the couch. "Lie on your back and hang your head at the edge of the couch."

She does just that and he puts his big, thick, long, hard cock in her throat and starts fucking her face hard and deep. She is taking it like a champ. He pushes his hard 9 inch cock balls deep until his ball sack hits her nose. Her saliva drips all over her face while he smacks her pussy lips and fingers her with his hooked fingers, hitting her G-spot. She is screaming with pleasure.

"Talk dirty to me!" she says.

"Shut up and take this big hard cock you nasty fuckin' cum slut!" he obliges.

He starts licking her pussy, swirling the tip of his tongue on her clit while he pumps his big hard cock in her throat. "You like that you fuckin' whore?"

"Yes daddy I love it!" she says.

He slaps her face and continues to fuck her throat hard and rough. Then he picks her up, turns her around and throws her back on the couch. He lifts her legs open and shoves his hard cock in her dripping wet pussy. He grabs her neck and chokes her as he fucks her. He loosens his grip only until her face turns red. She gasps for air. He slaps her. She is moaning as loud as she can. Their sweaty bodies writhe and rub against each other while they fuck like rabid animals.

"Oh fuck daddy I'm gonna cum!" she screams as she vigorously rubs her clit and squirts as her whole body shakes. He continues to fuck her balls deep, thrusting his big hard throbbing cock deeper and faster with every stroke.

He picks her up and turns her around so she is on her hands and knees. The ease with which he manhandles her is an extreme turn-on for her.

He gets down on his knees and shoves his face in her pussy from behind. He sticks his tongue inside her wet, warm juicy pussy and slides it up and down, licking her pussy juices. She moans with pleasure. He spits on her butthole and rubs it with his thumb and licks it. He then inserts his index finger in her ass to loosen it up a bit. She turns her head and looks directly in his eyes. He stands up and slowly puts his hard cock in her ass. She gasps for air and grabs on to his wrist. He pushes his cock halfway in her ass then slowly pulls it out. Then he puts it back in and this time two inches deeper and then pulls it out. The third time he pushes his cock balls deep. He grabs her hair and pulls on it hard as he starts fucking her ass hard, fast and deep. She screams with pleasure and pain.

"Take this cock in your ass you fuckin' nasty anal whore!" he shouts as he fucks her ass rough while pulling her hair. He then puts his fingers, like a fish hook, in her mouth and pulls on her cheek while he smacks her ass with the other hand. He then grabs her throat and chokes her as he fucks her ass.

"Ah fuck yes daddy! Oh fuck! Fuck me! Fuck my ass! It's yours!" she screams.

"Now suck on this cock whore." He pulls out his cock from her ass and she gets down on her knees. He shoves his cock deep in her throat and fucks her face. He holds her hair and pulls on it as she tries to push her face down his cock. He pulls out his cock and slaps her face with it before shoving it back in her throat. He grabs her head from the back and pushes it on his cock till she can't breathe and holds it there for a few seconds until she taps his thigh.

He pulls out his hard throbbing cock, picks her up in his arms and sits down on the couch. While holding her by her waist, he places her pussy directly over his cockhead and lowers her on his hard cock. He then lifts her up and back down on his cock, fucking her like she was feather-light. She places her hands on his hard chest muscles and she rides his big hard cock up and down, up and down, up and down, her ass cheeks slapping against his thighs. Her pussy juices are dripping all over his hard cock and balls. "Now suck my dick you dirty slut!"

She gets down on her knees in front of him and he holds her head and shoves his hard cock in her throat, making her choke and gag on his cock. He grabs her hair in a ponytail and lets her force her face down on his cock. She holds his cock shaft and tilts her head to the side so his cockhead pushes against her cheek and then pops it out of her mouth. He loves the cock-popping sound.

"Get back on my cock now!" he orders her.

She gets up and turns around so her back is towards him and sits her ass back on his cock. Her gaping ass hole takes his cock with ease. She screams with pleasure and pain and his big thick long hard cock stretches her ass while he holds her by the waist and fucks her ass balls deep. He pulls on her hair and her head tilts backwards as she rides his cock up and down. He spanks her ass repeatedly making it red with the other hand and squeezes her ass cheeks while he watches the beautiful and sexy sight of her ass bobbing up and down his big hard cock. She feels another orgasm approaching and starts to rub her clit.

"Oh fuck yes! Fuck my tight ass! I'm gonna cum baby! Oh fuck...Oh God yes! Ah fuck!!!" she screams as she rubs her clit and squirts all over her white couch and granite floor.

He lifts her off his cock and places her on the floor. "Get down on your hands and knees, arch your back and stick that ass up in the air."

She does just that and he spits in her gaping ass before shoving his big hard cock back inside her ass hole. She rests her face on the floor and spreads her ass cheeks open with both her hands as he fucks her ass balls deep. She is screaming with pleasure.

He spanks her ass hard and then pulls on her hair hard, lifting her head from the floor. He then places his right foot on the side of her face while he fucks her ass. "You like that big cock in your ass you slut?"

"Yes daddy I love it! This ass is yours! Use it and abuse it!" she replies.

He pushes her body down on the floor so she's now lying on her stomach and he's on top of her, fucking her ass hard, fast and deep. He leans his face on her face and licks the side of it while it's pressed against the floor. Then he puts two of his fingers in her mouth and sticks them down her throat and then hooks them on her cheek to stretch her mouth open.

He starts to moan louder now as he is about to cum too. He starts thrusting his hard cock harder, faster and deeper while his pelvis and upper thighs slap against her ass cheeks. "Aaahh I'm gonna cum baby!"

He pulls out his cock and stands up. She quickly gets up on her knees and turns around to face him. She grabs his hard cock and strokes it while looking straight into his eyes. She loves the expression of pleasure on his face as she strokes his cock waiting for him to shoot his big load of hot cum all over her wide open mouth and face.

"Aaarrrggghh fuck! Ah baby! I'm gonna cum! Take my big load of cum you nasty cum-guzzling slut...swallow every drop of it!" he shouts as he starts to shoot his warm thick cum all over her face.

She holds his cockhead directly above her open mouth so she can catch most of his cum. It's a big load and she loves it filling up her mouth. She squeezes the last drop of cum from his cockhead and licks the tip of his cock. She then gargles with it before she swallows it all. She looks up into his eyes, with her face covered with his cum and smiles.

3 YOLO TARGET

A young man walks into a Target to buy coffee. He is walking down an aisle when he crosses paths with a tall beautiful young woman with a big round ass. She is dressed in business casual attire with a white dress shirt and black pin-striped dress pants which are really accentuating her ass. They both look at each other and she smiles at him. She is on the phone as she walks past him and stops in front of him on the opposite side of the aisle, as if to get his attention. He pauses for a few seconds but carries on walking to find his coffee. He realizes that the girl might be trying to get his attention. After he has found his coffee, he decides to look for her in the store. So he walks past the aisles and looks for her in every aisle on his right, hoping to spot her. After a few aisles he finds her checking out utensils. He musters up all the courage he can, walks up to her and says, "I'm really nervous right now and don't usually do this, but I saw you and thought you were really hot and had to come say hi."

The girl starts to blush. "Oh wow! No one really does this anymore. I'm really flattered that you had the courage to come up to me. I really appreciate it."

He is now even hornier after witnessing this girl's

awesome personality. "Can I have your number?"

She replies, "Unfortunately I have a boyfriend."

"What about your SnapChat or Instagram?" he rebuts.

She hesitates a moment and says, "Sure you can follow me on Instagram."

She shares with him her Instagram username and he finds her on the app. "Maybe I will message you on there," he says. They both say their farewells and he goes on his way out.

This encounter has really made him excited yet a little nervous. He walks back to his car but can't stop thinking about the woman he just met. He checks out her Instagram profile and looks at all the sexy pictures she has posted in bikinis and dancing scantily clad in clubs. He really wants to fuck this girl. As he is swiping through her images, he sees her walk out of the Target. She walks to her car and opens her trunk to put in the shopping bags. He decides to walk up to her but thinks that it might seem creepy and maybe a little stalk-ish. But you only live once right? So he thinks what the hell has he got to lose. So he comes out of his car and walks up to her, but before getting too close, he exclaims, "Hi there."

She turns around and is pleasantly surprised by him. They both smile as they talk and he says, "I don't know if I should ask you this but what the hell. Would you like to go back to my car and sit in the backseat and chat?"

She replies, "Is that what you really want to do? Just chat?"

He laughs, "Maybe more?"

She closes her trunk. "Yeah sure"

He can't believe what just happened. He gets excited at the thought that he actually might get to fuck this girl right here right now in the backseat of his car. He has an instant erection and she notices the bulge in his pants as they walk to his car.

He opens the door for her and she sits inside. He walks to the other passenger door and sits in as well.

She says, "Your car smells nice."

And before she can say anything else, he leans over and kisses her luscious lips. They start making out passionately, licking and sucking on each other's lips as he gently nibbles and sucks on her juicy lower lip. His hands reach for her tits and discover how big and juicy they are. He starts to squeeze them and rub them over her white dress shirt as he slips his hand in and grabs her tits over her bra.

She unbuttons her shirt and unhooks her bra to reveal her tits. Her nipples are erect and he immediately puts his mouth on them and starts to suck them. She starts to moan and run her fingers through his hair as he squeezes and massages her juicy tits, licking, kissing and sucking them all over. She is getting extremely wet.

She pulls off his T-shirt to reveal his slim yet toned body and starts to touch his chest and stomach as he sucks her pink nipples with his soft, warm, wet mouth. He swirls his warm, wet, soft tongue around her nipples and she is dripping wet at this point. He takes off his pants and boxers and reveals his big, thick, long and hard cock and big juicy balls.

She grabs his hard cock and starts to stroke it as he goes back to kissing her luscious juicy lips. He reaches for her pants, unbuttons them and pulls them off. She is wearing these really cute white lace panties. He pulls them off and reveals a shaved bald pussy which is extremely wet at this point. He touches her soft, warm, wet pussy and gets even harder. He gets down on his knees in front of her, starts to kiss her inner thighs and then slides his warm, wet, soft tongue over her wet pussy lips. She starts to moan louder. He licks her clit up and down, up and down, swirling the tip of his tongue over her erect clit and she starts to quiver with pleasure. He licks her pussy for about 5 minutes and she starts to shake and orgasm, her whole body convulsing as if she's having a seizure. That turns him on even more and his cock is as hard as a rock at this point.

She tells him, "I want to suck that big hard cock of yours."

So he sits back and she leans over his hard cock and gives his mushroom-shaped cockhead a little lick. Then she puts his cock deep down her throat and gags on it a little.

She exclaims, "Oh wow! It's so big and hard right now. I can't wait for it to be inside my tight, wet, young pussy."

She starts to suck his dick deeper and faster while rubbing his balls. Then she licks and sucks his shaved balls as she moans. They are both ready to fuck each other's brains out. So she climbs on top of him and guides his big hard cock to her extremely wet pussy and sits on it till it hits her insides. "Ah fuck that dick feels so good inside my pussy," she exclaims.

He grabs her round juicy ass, squeezes both her ass cheeks and helps her ride his big hard cock up and down, up and down, up and down, her ass slapping against his thighs. He sucks her tits and nipples as she is riding his big hard cock. He tells her to turn around so he can fuck her reverse cowgirl position. She turns around, arches her back and he rubs his cockhead on her pussy lips and clit before shoving it back inside her wet warm juicy pussy. They both moan as he fucks her hard while grabbing her ass cheeks and smacking them. She moans louder as he spanks her ass. Her sexy ass jiggles as she moves up and down his hard throbbing cock.

"Oh my God I'm going to cum again," she moans and squeezes her ass cheeks over his big hard cock and starts to cum. "Oh baby your cock feels so good inside me!"

She cums all over his hard cock and balls, as he grabs her juicy tits, squeezes them, gently twisting her nipples with his fingers. After she has orgasmed a second time, she gets off his hard cock and puts it back into her warm, wet mouth. Her juicy luscious soft lips wrap around the shaft of his hard cock and make him feel like he is going to explode. He grabs her hair in a ponytail as she tries to deepthroat his cock. She manages to put only four inches of it down her throat until she gags. He cannot take the pleasure anymore.

He shouts, "I'm gonna cum baby! Oh God baby…I'm gonna cum!"

He grabs her head and pushes his cock deeper in her throat and starts to cum in her mouth. She keeps sucking his cock as he squirts his big load of warm cum inside her mouth. She opens her mouth slightly and lets the cum drip out of her mouth onto his hard cock and balls. She keeps sucking his sensitive cock and cock head as he keeps moaning and quivering with extreme ecstasy. She pulls out his cock from her mouth and starts to lick his cum off his balls and shaft of his cock.

He just tilts his head back and is in heaven. He grabs the Kleenex box and hands it to her. She cleans her mouth and then cleans his cock and balls off the big load of cum. They both laugh as they get dressed.

He says, "I'm Juan by the way."

She shakes his hand, smiles and says, "Nice to meet you Juan."

4 SAVAGE BOSS

It's April's second week at this multinational corporation and she is very grateful to have landed this great job. She had been looking for a job for almost 4 months. She has been proving herself to be a great new employee at the company and people are noticing. Her job position is the new Payroll Administrator and she gets to work at the 53rd floor of this skyscraper in the middle of Manhattan. She moved from Oklahoma City for this position so it's even more special for her – leaving her semi-country living for the posh Manhattan lifestyle. She can't wait to get her first paycheck so she can explore NYC.

So far everyone at her new job seems to like her. She is getting along fine with everyone at the office and she's also got a great view from her desk overlooking the Manhattan skyline. One of the biggest perks she feels of this new job is that the CEO of the company is handsome. He has this daddy look with salt and pepper hair and a great body for his late-forties age. She was interviewed by him as well and she couldn't get her eyes off of him in his business suit and an air of success and domination. She was trying so hard not to imagine seeing him naked and being dominated by him. She would totally let him use her body any way he wanted. But she also must be careful as to not have any workplace romances because she really likes this new job and doesn't want to jeopardize it in any way. She actually met her last boyfriend at her last job and it got pretty messy after the breakup. Hopefully she can maintain a good working relationship with her boss and still have a secret crush on him.

Her work has been pretty hectic lately for her since it's the end of the month and she has to get the company payroll in order. She's been working long hours every day. It looks like she might have to stay a few extra hours today. She doesn't mind it though because she likes the peace and quiet of the empty office and she loves the view of the city lights from up here.

Everyone in the office has left and she gets up to get a glass of water in the lunch room. As she is sipping on her glass of water, she notices the light on in her boss's office.

"Hmmm. I didn't know he was still here," she thinks.

She goes back to her desk. A few minutes later, her desk phone rings. She is startled by it and picks up the phone.

"Hello?" she asks.

"Hi April! This is Joshua. Can you please come into my office?" her boss speaks on the other end.

"Sure. I'll be right there."

She knocks on her boss's door and is told to come in. Joshua's fingers are on his temple and he is looking down intently at some papers on his desk.

"Hey. Come on in April. Please take a seat," he points at the chair in front of him. "There seems to be some discrepancy in the payroll numbers this month. Can you please take a look and tell me what's going on?"

"Oh sure let me take a look." She is handed the papers and she flips through them. "Oh I see it! There is a typo here." She walks to his side of the desk, puts the papers in front of him and points to the typographical error.

"Ah I see. Well luckily it's just a typo. Please make sure

you fix it before you leave tonight and adjust the numbers in the system accordingly," he looks up at her while handing back the papers. "By the way, I love the smell of your perfume. What is it?"

"Oh thank you Sir! It is Chloe," she responds while smiling and adjusting her cleavage.

His gaze locks on her cleavage. She notices.

"Is there anything else Sir?"

"No that will be all April. And you don't have to call me Sir all the time. Joshua will do just fine."

"Oh ok sure Joshua." She walks back to her desk all flustered and feeling a little horny.

She goes about fixing the typo and updating the payroll files in the system but can't stop thinking about her encounter with her boss and how confidently he flirted with her. She is turned on and is thinking of all kinds of scenarios in her head. She starts wishfully thinking that her boss calls her in his office and then fucks the shit out of her on his big desk. As she is fantasizing, her phone rings again.

"April, when you're done with the numbers, please fetch me the wine opener from the lunch room."

"Sure. I'll be right over." She grabs the wine opener from the lunchroom and knocks on her boss's door.

There is a bottle of wine sitting on his desk. Only his desk lamp is on with the ceiling lights off. His tie is loosened around his neck but he is still wearing his suit.

"Please join me April. Have a little glass of this cabernet with me."

She obediently sits down while he uncorks the bottle.

"Tell me April. How do you like working for this company?"

"I'm really enjoying it. I am grateful to have been given this opportunity."

"You're welcome April. There is a lot of room for growth here. An ambitious girl like you is sure to climb the corporate ladder quickly." He pours a glass and hands it to her.

They both sip on the wine and chit chat about a multitude of things. There is laughter. There is some flirting. They both are feeling a little more uninhibited.

She notices a piece of black fabric on his desk. She picks it up.

"Oh my God! Is this a blindfold?" She laughs as she figures out what it is. "What do you use this for?"

He stands up and walks to her side of the desk. He takes the blindfold from her. "Let me show you."

Her heart starts to race. He stands behind her, places the blindfold on her eyes and ties it behind her head.

"Oh my God this is crazy!" she exclaims as he takes the glass of wine from her hand and sets it on the desk.

"Just relax and let go April."

"Do you do this with all your new hires Joshua?"

"Only the ones I want to promote April."

They both laugh.

She feels like she can trust him. She wants to trust him completely. She wants to submit herself to her billionaire boss. She immediately starts to get wet and he hasn't even touched her yet.

"Do you trust me April?"

"Strangely I do."

"Good! Just play along! You're just getting your Christmas bonus a little earlier this year."

She hears him clear the top of his desk and then gently touches her hand. He holds her hand and directs her to stand up. He then gently grabs her by her waist and directs her to sit on the desk. Every little touch of his sends direct signals to her pussy to start juicing.

"Now lean back and lie down," he says.

She lies down on her back on the top of his desk. She has no idea what is going to happen next but she is willing to give him full control of the moment.

He opens his drawer and takes two pairs of handcuffs out. She hears something clinking but has no idea what it is. He holds her left wrist up, places the cold shiny metal handcuff on it and locks it.

"Oh shit! Is that what I think it is?" she asks.

"Shhh. Don't speak," he replies.

He places the other handcuff on her right wrist. She wonders where the other end of those handcuffs will lock on to. Her heart is racing and she is getting even wetter with excitement and anticipation. He gently takes off her shoes. He then gently slides his hand up her leg, caressing it until he reaches for her pantyhose under her skirt and rolls it right off her leg. He does the same with the other leg. Her mouth opens up slightly and she starts to sigh with pleasure. He then holds both her ankles and spreads her legs open. She gasps for air.

"Give me your hands," he commands.

She stretches her arms out for him to hold. He then handcuffs her wrists to her ankles so she is technically holding on to her ankles, helping her legs spread open. Her skirt is still on but unbuttoned and wrapped around her waist.

He then gets on the desk in front of her and slides both his hands all the way from her ankles to her calves and inner thighs. He reaches her crotch and rubs her pussy from over her panties.

"Wow you're so wet already," he says.

"You make me wet Joshua," she replies.

He reaches for a pair of scissors and gently slides the tip of it along her bare legs and inner thighs. The sensation of the sharp cold metal against her smooth soft skin excites her. She has never felt this combination of sensations before. It's a cocktail of pleasure, excitement, anticipation, intrigue, fear and confusion and she loves it.

He slips the open scissor blades under the side of her panties and snips them. She sighs with anticipation and excitement. In one swift motion, he pulls the snipped panties and throws them over his shoulders on the floor. He then takes the scissors and gently caresses her dripping wet pussy with the cold shiny metal blades. She suddenly gasps for air. He puts the scissors aside and leans over her wet, warm, juicy pussy and gently blows on it.

"Oh fuck that feels good," she says and then laughs.

"You like that?" he asks.

"Yes very much…I am feeling all these sensations that I've never felt before. And this blindfold is intensifying the whole experience."

"That's the whole point of the blindfold baby."

As he continues blowing gently on her wet, warm pussy, his lips gently lean further in and kiss her pussy lips. Opening his mouth slightly, he sticks his tongue out and licks her clit.

"Oh my fuckin' God! Fuck that feels so fuckin' good!" she exclaims.

All this while her ankles are handcuffed to her wrists which are helping her spread her own legs wide open for him to explore her pussy and whatever else he wants. The whole submission aspect of this experience is driving her insane with pleasure. She has never been so dripping wet.

He slides his soft, warm, wet tongue up and down her wet, warm pussy lips making her pussy even wetter. He swirls the tip of his tongue on her clit and gently rubs it up and down and in circular motions making her moan with extreme ecstasy. She begins to shake and quiver as she cums explosively for the first time of the night. Her whole body convulses as she orgasms.

He uses his thumb and index finger to press her clit hood upwards so her engorged clit is fully revealed and then licks it with varying pressures of his tongue. He increases the pressure and tempo of his licks until he sees her body start to shake and convulse again and then slows the tempo and pressure of his tongue. She cums again.

"Oh God baby that feels so good! Aaahh fuck! Aaahh!" she moans.

"Good baby! Cum for me! Cum for me baby! Cum!" he says in a seductive tone.

She cums again and again. He then starts to finger her while continuing to lick her clit. As soon as he inserts two of his fingers in her wet warm pussy, she gasps. He then hooks them and starts rubbing her G-spot. Within minutes she starts to shake and tremble and experiences a whole body orgasm again.

"Baby no one has ever made me cum like this," she admits.

"And no one ever will," he replies.

He then gets up and walks over to her head. He holds her by her shoulders and pulls her so her neck is over the edge.

"Let your head hang loose over the edge of the desk," he says in a commanding voice.

She does just that. He then pulls off her blindfold.

"Oh wow that view is incredible," she says in wonderment as she looks over the 53rd level night view of the inverted Manhattan skyline.

"Keep looking at the view," he says and walks over to her pussy and starts licking and fingering her again. She shakes, trembles and convulses as she cums yet again.

"Fuck! Aaahh fuck baby…aaaaahh fuck yes…Yes! Aaaahh fuck I'm cumming!" she screams as she has the biggest orgasm of the night.

5 UBER THIRST TRAP

Edward loves coming to this park every day, parking his car in front of this beautiful sycamore tree and having his breakfast before starting his shift as an Uber driver. He has been coming to this park for three years now, ever since he moved to this town from his old place 45 miles away. This is a much more peaceful side of the city. This park is especially nice. It is quite big and has some amazing hiking trails on the hills. He sometimes takes a nap in his car after breakfast or lunch, since it is so quiet that you can only hear the leaves rustling gently in the breeze.

It is time for him to go online on his Uber app and start working. He loves driving for Uber as it gives him the freedom to be his own boss and make as much or as little money as he wants when he wants. He is grateful for this new digital age and the sharing economy. There are so many apps available now where anyone can make money on the side or a full-time income with just their smartphones. Just merely eleven years ago, before the first iPhone came out, you couldn't dream of doing the things you can do now with your phone. Sharing economy apps came much later. Maybe only five years ago. It's a great time that we all live in.

He opens his Uber driver app and goes online, waiting for his first trip. Every day for him is an adventure. He just doesn't know who he will pick up and where he will take them.

He receives a trip request and starts driving towards the pickup location. The location is only 1 mile away. He arrives and picks up this young Asian girl. She comes and sits in the front. Usually young girls don't sit in the front when the driver is an older male. But when they do, it usually means they want to converse.

Ed greets her and she responds graciously. They do a little small talk. He finds out that she was just dropping off a Turo car. Turo is a new smartphone app that lets you rent privately owned cars within a certain radius that you specify. It is regular people renting their personal cars just like in AirBnB people rent their homes for short or long periods of time. She is now being dropped off to her workplace.

It is just like any other Uber trip until this young girl starts asking some interesting questions.

She asks him, "So what's the craziest experience you've had in Uber?"

Now he gets asked this question quite a bit. So he goes on to share his experience of some drunk guy who was passed out in his car one night and wouldn't get out at his destination.

So the girl replies, "My question was actually of a sexual nature."

"Oh I see," he replies. "Well I have met a couple of girls that I ended up dating."

"But what about a girl doing something sexual to you during a live Uber trip?"

Edward laughs and replies, "Hahaha…no…nothing sexual has happened while I was driving a customer to her location."

"Really? Hmmm."

"Yes really. But I'm open to it for sure."

They both laugh. Edward has a feeling that this young girl wants to experience exactly what she is inquiring about. So he asks her, "Why do you ask? Would you be interested in experiencing something like that?"

She smiles and responds, "Maybe."

Edward has just gotten an instant erection. Uber is very strict when it comes to the dealings between passengers and drivers. There is a zero tolerance policy in sexual harassment incidents. Drivers can get fired instantly and lose their driving privileges. Or much worse can happen if the passenger feels the need to sue the driver or Uber on sexual harassment charges or rape. Needless to say, that is extremely serious business. But in that moment, as he is thinking about all that, he makes a split second decision. He decides to take a very big risk.

He recalls a famous quote by Nietzsche: "The secret of reaping the greatest fruitfulness and the greatest enjoyment from life is to live dangerously."

He holds the girl's hand and puts it on his erection.

She grabs his hard cock and is pleasantly surprised, "Oh my God, you are already so hard."

"Well all this sexual talk got me horny," he replies.

"Well pull it out."

They are driving on the freeway and there is another 15 minutes to the destination. He unbuttons and unzips his pants, takes off his boxers and pulls out his hard cock. The girl grabs his cock and starts rubbing it. It is broad daylight and it's around 11:30am. They are both pretty nervous but also very excited at what is happening right now.

She starts to stroke his hard cock while looking out her window nervously. "Oh my God, I hope no one sees this."

He takes his dress shirt off that he is wearing on top of a T-shirt and covers his cock with it. But truck and SUV drivers will still be able to look in and see a big bulge under the shirt and a girl stroking that bulge. It is very risky behavior when it comes to driver/passenger safety of a moving vehicle, as well as inappropriate workplace behavior. But these two are living on the edge and experiencing a once-in-a-lifetime fantasy come true.

She grabs his hard cock, strokes it and rubs his balls. She exclaims, "Wow it is so big."

He smiles and says, "I'm glad you like it."

"Wait…it is too dry. I need some lotion in my hands."

"Why don't you just suck it instead?"

"No way!" she says and continues to stroke his cock. With the vacant hand, she reaches in her purse and pulls out a lotion bottle. She squirts some on her stroking hand and starts to rub his hard throbbing cock and balls.

He starts to moan. "Oh my God it feels so good. I can't believe I'm getting a hand job from a passenger in broad daylight while I'm dropping her to work."

They both laugh.

Her freeway exit is quickly approaching and she says, "Cum already…I'm almost at work."

"Ok I'm almost there. Ah! Fuck this feels so wrong and so good." He starts moaning louder.

She starts stroking faster and faster. She can feel his throbbing veins sliding against her palm and she is getting really turned on.

He tries to touch her leg. But she quickly shrugs his hand away and says, "Don't touch me. I just want to jack you off."

"Ok. But can I have your number so I can see you again?" he asks.

"No this is just a one-time thing," she replies.

He doesn't care. He is enjoying his one-time hand job. He takes the exit. And just as he is exiting the freeway, he starts to cum. "Oh fuck I'm gonna cum. Aaahh! Aaaahh! Aaarrgghh! Fuck! Aaaarrrggghh!"

He shoots his big load of hot cum all over her hand and she keeps stroking and stroking. She wants to make sure she squeezes every drop of cum from his big, thick, long and hard cock.

She wipes her hand with his shirt that was covering his

cock. And they arrive at her destination. As she is getting out of the car, she turns to him and says, "If you want a blowjob later on tonight, call me."

"Oh now you want to give me your number. I'm not complaining. Fuck yes I would love a blowjob from you." They exchange phone numbers. She finally tells him her name. He saves it in his phone as 'Susan (Uber rider BJ).'

She gets out of the car and says, "Happy Valentine's Day!"

"Same to you Susie." He had no idea it was Valentine's Day. He drives off with the biggest smile on his face, thinking about how Susie's mouth would feel on his hard cock tonight.

6 AIRPLANE AF

Elijah has just arrived at the airport only an hour before his flight back home. He has had an amazing time with his cousins at the cottage by the lake in upstate New York. It was his first time in New York and he made sure he made the most of the five days he was there. He got to see the famous Time Square. He couldn't go to the Statue of Liberty but there is only so much you can do in five days. He is glad to have had the experience and has gotten enough taste of the place to keep coming back. He fondly reminisces the time he has spent the last few days while standing in the TSA queue.

His flight time is swiftly arriving and he is thinking he might not make it. There are maybe about fifteen people ahead of him. He is getting nervous and fidgety. Just five people ahead of him in the same line is this really hot girl wearing tight yoga pants that are really making her ass accentuate into a fantastic shape of deliciousness. Elijah is an ass man for as long as he can remember. Growing up he would look at old Cosmopolitan magazines and flip to the women's underwear ads. He would masturbate to those women in white lace bras and panties. He even had this English teacher in middle school who would wear these tight pants that would make her round juicy ass pop out. He would fantasize touching his teacher's ass accidentally somehow and would think of scenarios of how he could make that happen.

He realizes he just went on this random daydream adventure and quickly focuses back on reality. He glances at his watch and there is only thirty minutes left till the plane leaves. He is getting nervous but the view of this girl's ass is helping him distract himself from the impending predicament. What an ass she has. "Thank God for yoga pants," he thinks to himself.

During all this nervousness and excitement, he suddenly hears an announcement that his flight is delayed by thirty minutes. "Oh what a fuckin' relief!" he thinks. That relaxes him.

It's the hot girl's turn through the fully body security scanner. He finally gets a good look at her from behind. She has amazing straight brown hair with a sheen you don't see every day. They reach her lower back. She is not too tall, maybe about 5' 4." She lifts her arms for the security guy to wave his wand around her and that lifts her T-shirt up from the back. He can see a tramp stamp on her lower back. "That's fuckin' hot," he whispers under his breath.

She turns around to put her stuff in those plastic containers for the scanner and he finally sees her face. She isn't a Kate Beckinsale but she is most certainly a cutie. He would give her maybe a solid 7 out of 10, which is great because he considers himself a 7 too. What she lacks (as they say) in her face, she certainly makes up for in her beautifully sculpted ass cheeks. Just like every guy's dream, he hopes she would be the one to sit next to him in the plane. But that never happens, ever. It is always either an old fat lady who sleeps even before the plane has taken off and farts the whole flight through, or some big, husky, hairy plumber who hasn't discovered deodorants yet.

Elijah finally gets on the plane and puts his carry-on in

the overhead compartment. He sits down on his aisle seat and looks at the two empty seats to his left. He starts praying, "Please God let that hot girl with that perfect ass come sit next to me. Please!" He patiently waits and looks at everyone that walks past him in the aisle. The girl is nowhere to be seen. He thinks that it's never going to happen so he might as well put his headphones on and close his eyes. Someone taps his shoulder and he opens his eyes and it's an old fat lady. "Oh God no!" he whispers. He gets up from his seat to let her in to her window seat. "Thank God she's at least not right next to me," he thinks. Before sitting back down on his seat, he pans the airplane to see where that hot chick is. He can't find her but he does notice how empty this flight is going back to Los Angeles. He sits back down. The plane takes off.

He wakes up from his short nap and realizes there is still an empty seat on his left. "Thank God I don't have to smell the lady's farts," he thinks as he glances over to her and smiles. He realizes she is not the stereotypical old fat lady that he so often encounters. She seems very sweet and well-kempt. She is even wearing a young-woman perfume. He gets up to go use the lavatory. As he is walking down the aisle, he sees the hot brunette with the ass sitting just three rows of seats behind him in a window seat. He smiles at her as he walks past her and she smiles back. "Yes!" he whispers.

On his way back from the lavatory, he notices she has two empty seats next to her. He grabs this opportunity and walks up to her and says, "Hi…excuse me…hi I'm Elijah," he extends his hand to shake hers.

She shakes his hand and says, "Hi Elijah, I'm Susan."

"Are these two seats vacant?"

She nods. "Yes they are, so far."

"Would you mind terribly if I sit on this aisle seat?"

"Not at all…in fact, I wouldn't mind some company on this six hour flight."

"That is just great. Thank you so much." He sits down

on the seat, with a seat still empty between them.

They both get to talking and sharing their trip experience in New York. She is a makeup artist and an aspiring actress like almost every other girl in LA. But that's ok. He just wants to fuck her and maybe have a friend-with-benefits arrangement. She seems to respond really well to everything that he says. He thinks he just might be able to get her phone number by the end of the flight and set up a date with this hot sexy thing. The conversation moves along smoothly. She starts to adjust her bra straps every now and then which he finds so sexy. She explains to him how her boobs are too big for her body. He glances at them and replies that they really aren't, all the while thinking to himself, "Fuck! Your tits are so delicious; I want to bury my face in them." The conversation starts getting a little flirtatious and sexual. He admits that he has always wanted to join the Mile High Club but has never had the opportunity.

She replies, "Oh my God! Me too!"

He continues, "Well would you be open to exploring the possibility of us joining the Mile High Club together?"

She laughs and says, "If you play your cards right Elijah, I just might agree."

That reply has just given him an instant rock hard boner. She looks straight at his crotch and smiles.

He catches her looking at the bulge in his pants and leans over to whisper to her, "Would you like to touch it?"

She smiles and says, "Do you want to join me in the restroom?"

"Fuck yeah I do."

She gets up first and goes into the restroom. He waits for a minute, gets up and looks around to see if anyone is looking. He then goes to the restroom door and knocks on the door.

She whispers, "Come in."

This plane isn't a really small one but is no Airbus A380 either. The lavatory has just enough space for both of them up close. So it pretty much is ideal for two people fucking in a couple of different positions only.

She shuts the toilet seat cover, sits on it facing him and unbuttons his pants. It is that part of the flight where the airplane cabin lights are dimmed for people to take a nap so they know there won't be a lot of disturbance. But they also have to make this relatively quick. His big hard cock plops out of his boxers and she immediately gobbles it like a pro. She starts sucking his hard cock and making those slurping and slight throat-choking sounds. This makes him even harder. He holds her head with both his hands, while she grabs both his ass cheeks and he starts thrusting his pelvis back and forth, back and forth, pumping his big thick long and hard cock in and out of her mouth. She squeezes his ass cheeks, and slaps one of them, to which he whispers, "Shh"

She pulls him back and forth into her mouth and throat until his cock is dripping wet with her saliva. She gives his balls a few licks and sucks. He then sits on the toilet seat cover while she pulls down her yoga pants to her ankles revealing her three day old pubic hair growth and an extremely pretty looking and dripping wet pussy.

He rubs her pussy a little and whispers, "Oh my God you are so fuckin' wet."

She sits on top of him and guides his big hard cock into her primed pussy. He immediately moans at the warmth and slippery wetness of her tight pussy. He grabs both her ass cheeks with both his hands and helps her ass up and down, up and down, up and down his hard cock. Her wet, warm, juicy pussy lips wrap around his big thick long and hard throbbing cock and her pussy juices flow out and all over his balls. She is creaming all over his hard cock as she rides it up and down, up and down, faster and faster. They are careful enough to not make a lot of flesh-slapping sounds as their bodies collide in coitus.

At that very moment, someone pulls on the lavatory door lever and they both stop moving instantaneously.

They both look at each other wide-eyed, wait for ten seconds, smile and then start fucking again. They've been at it for about seven minutes so far, which is about average for someone taking a crap. So there shouldn't be any suspicion raised. In fact, Elijah was just reading a Quora answer on his phone earlier about what happens if you are caught having sex in a plane. A flight attendant had answered that it's not forbidden or illegal as long as it is not in plain sight or sound.

He wants to fuck her from behind now while standing. He helps her to get up off his cock, stands up and turns her around. She puts one hand on the wall on her left and the other on the sink, looks back at him and sticks her ass out.

"Oh what a fuckin' hot ass you got girl," he whispers then rubs his hard cock head in between her wet pussy lips and clit before shoving it deep inside her pussy. He grabs her perfect juicy ass cheeks, spreads them open with both his hands and then starts to really fuck her hard and deep, still making sure her ass doesn't slap too hard against his body. She reaches from under her pussy, in between her legs and grabs his big juicy balls as he fucks her from behind. He is loving the sight and feel of his shiny wet hard cock sliding in and out, in and out, in and out of her extremely wet, warm, juicy pussy.

"Aaaahhhh fuck I'm gonna cum," he whispers.

She whispers, "Not yet please…just give me a minute." She starts rubbing her clit as he is fucking her. "Yes just like that baby. Yes I'm gonna cum too."

He starts fucking her deeper so she can feel his hard cock hit her insides.

She gasps for air vend rubs her clit faster. "Fuck fuck fuck. Yes yes yes," she whispers. "Oh fuck I'm cumming," as her legs start to shake.

This makes him uncontrollably horny and he whispers, "I'm gonna cum too. Fuck! Aaaaaahhhhh!"

They both cum simultaneously. He keeps pumping her

pussy as he is shooting his big warm load of cum inside her pussy. His cum filling up her pussy is adding to the warmth and gooey wetness of her pussy. He pumps a few more times and then pulls his cock out. "Are you on birth control?" he asks.

She nods.

"Oh thank God!" he whispers.

They both sigh and catch their breath. They wipe themselves off, pull up their pants, fix their hair real quick and walk out together, not caring about who sees them. They've already done the deed. They have successfully joined the Mile High Club together without getting caught. All they want to do now is get to their seats and take a nap before the plane lands. They both sit down and lean in for their first kiss. The kiss is passionate. They both giggle. Elijah wraps his arms around Susan as she rests her head on his chest and they both close their eyes with big smiles on their faces.

7 DUCK FACE RIDERS

Julia and her best friend Chrissie are taking selfies in Julia's bathroom mirror as they pout with their luscious pink lips and stick their round and toned sexy, hot asses out. They are both wearing the shortest dresses they had in their wardrobes. They both workout regularly at the same gym and have the most perfect bodies girls can have in their mid-twenties. With just enough of their abdomen showing their belly rings on their tanned skin, they both look incredibly sexy and ripe for sexual activity. Julia has slightly bigger tits than Chrissie, but Chrissie's tits are perkier like those of an 18 year old. When they are done taking SnapChat videos on their phones, they both scream, "Lets party!" and head out their front door.

A black Uber Escalade with dark tinted windows is waiting for them right in front to take them to their favorite club in Hollywood. They jump in the back of the SUV and greet the Uber driver named Kent. They both look at each other and Chrissie silently mouths the words, "He's hot" to Julia and they giggle. The ride is about an hour to the club and Julia asks him if he has an AUX cable for an iPhone.

He is properly equipped and hands it over to her and

says, "Here you go."

"Ooo someone is fully equipped and ready for the job," says Julia and all three of them laugh.

The air in the big black SUV has suddenly become sexual. Kent compliments the girls, "You both look really hot back there."

The girls respond gratefully and Chrissie says, "So do you Kent."

The girls giggle.

He asks if they are both single. Julia says she is seeing someone but it's not serious and Chrissie admits that she has a friend with benefits but no boyfriend. Julia asks him what his craziest experience has been while driving for Uber. He has had a few and starts to describe one of them to the girls. The incident is about picking up a really drunk passenger. But the girls want to know a crazy sexual experience that he might have had with one of the passengers. He admits he never has had any crazy sexual experiences before but would definitely be open to it. The girls look at each other, wink and smile.

Chrissie initiates the physical contact with him by leaning over and touching his strong muscular bicep and exclaims, "Wow you're strong Kent."

He smiles.

Only about ten minutes into the drive, Julia asks him if he could stop at a 7-Eleven on the way and he finds one and pulls up. The girls walk into the store and buy some gum. They both are feeling very naughty tonight as they had a few drinks before leaving their place. They walk out and Chrissie sits in the front passenger seat this time while Julia sits in the back. He is about to drive away when Chrissie puts her hand on his muscular thigh and gently rubs it. He is taken aback a little. Chrissie explains, "We really like you Kent, both Julia and I, and we wanted to ask you if you could help us out tonight."

He replies, "Sure how can I help?"

Chrissie says, "Well we have always talked about being

in a threesome with someone but haven't met a nice enough guy to have one with. But we think you are perfect for it."

He is surprised to hear that but obviously very excited because the girls are really sexy. "Ok but where are we going to do this? And don't you have to be at the club?"

Chrissie says, "Well the only reason we were going to the club was to get laid. So since we have already met a hot guy who is open-minded and adventurous, we would like to fuck your brains out. So can you park behind the 7-Eleven? Your car's backseat is big enough for all of us and your tints are pretty dark."

His heart begins racing with excitement and he obviously agrees and parks behind the 7-Eleven.

Chrissie jumps in the backseat and he follows. The girls sit on each side of him in the big backseat of the Escalade and Julia is the first one to place her hand on the side of his face, turns his head towards her and starts kissing him passionately.

He holds her neck and then slides his hand on to her juicy tits, starts rubbing and squeezing them while sucking on her lower lip and gently nibbling on it.

Meanwhile Chrissie rubs his dick from over his pants with one hand while unbuttoning his dress shirt with the other. She takes his shirt off and starts to kiss and lick his nipples while she unbuttons his pants.

He helps her take his pants off. He then turns to Chrissie and kisses her luscious soft pink lips and their tongues meet each other, swirling the tips, sucking on each other's lips and gently nibbling on them. He moves his lips to Chrissie's neck and kisses and licks it then reaches for her earlobe and sucks on it. He takes her shirt and bra off and reveals her beautiful tits. While he rubs and squeezes one of them, he sucks on her other nipple. He swirls the tip of his tongue in circles around her nipple and gently nibbles on it.

Julia is now stroking his big hard cock and rubbing his

balls while she enjoys the sight of her best friend being pleasured by this handsome stranger. She kneels down on the floor of the SUV and licks the tip of his big mushroom head before slowly taking the full length of his cock in her throat. She gasps for air, sighs, and puts it back in her throat deeper. She starts gagging on his big dick and loves it. She then puts his big juicy balls in her warm, wet mouth and sucks on them, licking all over his ball sack. He is in rapture!

Both the girls are on the floor now sucking his cock. Julia licks and sucks his balls while Chrissie sucks on his shaft. They switch positions and Julia deepthroats his big hard throbbing cock and feels his cockhead reach down her throat. She drools all over his dick as she pulls it out of her mouth. The girls start kissing while still playing with his dick and balls.

Julia gets up from the floor, pulls her thong to the side, holds his wet, throbbing, rock hard cock and rubs his perfectly-shaped cockhead on her extremely wet, warm and juicy pussy lips and clit. She then slowly guides it inside her and pushes her ass all the way down to his balls. She gasps as she feels her pussy being filled by his big, thick, long and hard cock, as she kisses his mouth.

He grabs her round, juicy ass with both his hands, spreads her ass cheeks and helps her ride his dick up and down, up and down, up and down, faster and harder with every stroke.

Chrissie licks his balls as he is fucking Julia.

Julia starts to moan louder and louder as she is about to cum. She squeezes her ass cheeks and pelvis on his dick as she gets closer and closer to having an orgasm. The thrill of having sex in public is making them all very excited. Julia moans loud as she cums and kisses him passionately, while she clinches her pussy tightly around his big hard dick.

It's Chrissie's turn now. Julia gets off his dick and Chrissie puts it in her mouth and tastes Julia's pussy juices.

She licks his shaft all around and licks his balls, then shoves it down her throat all the way to his balls. She turns around so she can fuck him in reverse cowgirl position. The sight of her perfectly toned ass excites him and makes him even harder. She turns her head and looks straight into his eyes as she lowers her ass on to his hard throbbing cock.

He guides his dick inside Chrissie's dripping wet, warm pussy and she moans and gasps for air as her tight pussy is barely able to fit his big dick. He grabs her ass cheeks with both his hands and squeezes them and then spanks them as she moans louder and tells him to do it again. She likes it rough and that makes him even more excited. Julia grabs and rubs his balls as he is fucking Chrissie. He grabs Chrissie's tits with both his hands and squeezes them hard and then squeezes her nipples with his fingers and thumbs. He grabs her hair and pulls on it and she screams with pleasure and starts riding his dick harder, faster and deeper, hitting her perfect ass cheeks on his thighs and pelvis. They both get really excited and get closer to cumming. He starts fucking her harder and faster while he places his hand on her neck and squeezes it. She is loves it. The sound of her ass slapping against his thighs and pelvis gets louder and they both start to moan louder.

Chrissie shouts, "I'm gonna cum! I'm gonna cum! Oh my God yes, yes, yes, oh God yes!" and cums all over his big hard throbbing dick.

He moans louder and can't control himself and is about to cum inside of her.

She shouts, "Yes baby you can cum inside me I'm on birth control."

And at that very moment, he shoots his big warm load of cum inside her.

She shouts, "Oh fuck I can feel your big hot load of cum filling my pussy up…oh fuck yes."

They both take a moment to catch their breath before all three of them start laughing about this whole experience that none of them will ever forget for the rest of their lives.

8 POLICE FINESSE

The night is young. The sky is clear. The air is fresh and cool. The top of Mary's convertible Mustang is down and she's driving along the winding mountain road to watch tonight's Geminid's meteor shower. She has been newly single and this day for her is the mark of a new beginning. None of her friends are astronomy lovers like her so she decided to come watch the spectacular display of flying burning rocks in the night sky by herself. She has watched previous meteor showers from atop the cliff that she's driving on. It's the best vantage point because it's always dark and desolate here with no street lights.

No one's on the road in front of her or behind her so she decides to press on the gas a little. She's listening to the Roadhouse Blues by The Doors - one of her favorite bands. The wind is blowing through her hair and she's a little high on weed which makes the whole experience just a little more enjoyable. She can't wait to arrive at her spot. It's at the top of the cliff where a big old tree log lies on its side making it the perfect makeshift bench overlooking the ocean as its waves hit the bottom of the cliff and that's the only sound you hear. You can see the coastal lights of the beaches from up here.

As she is envisioning her spot in her mind, she is oblivious to the fact that she's driving pretty fast but just as she realizes that, she hears the sound of police sirens blaring behind her with red and blue light flooding the darkness.

"Fuck fuck fuck! I'm such a fuckin' idiot!" she shouts. She pulls over to the side and waits anxiously for her fate. The cop walks up to her car and asks for her driver's license and registration. She turns her head to look at the cop and is taken aback by how handsome this cop is. She gets flustered not because she is going to get a speeding ticket but because of the cop's hotness. She smiles at him flirtatiously as she hands him her license and registration and says, "Here you go officer. Is there anything else I can give you...if you catch my drift that is?"

The officer replies, "Ma'am I am an officer of the law. What exactly are you hinting at here?"

"Oh nothing officer…I'm just being nice,"

"Do you know why I stopped you?"

"Is it because I'm attractive?"

"No ma'am. I stopped you because you were 20 miles over the speed limit," he replies with a straight face.

"I'm sorry officer. I'm just trying to get to a spot where I can watch the meteor shower before it's too late. Please don't give me a ticket. I'll do anything to avoid getting a ticket,"

"Well just follow the law to avoid getting a ticket Ma'am,"

"Ok officer. I will do that from now on. But can you please not give me a speeding ticket this time? As you can see I have a clean record,"

"Ma'am I can't help you with that,"

She pouts and gently rubs her tits over her top. "Are you sure officer?"

The cop looks at her tits and gets excited a little but pretends he isn't. "Ma'am what are you doing?"

She looks down at her tits. "Oh this? Nothing

officer…my breasts are just itchy…just scratching them that's all. That's not against the law now is it?”

“No ma'am that's not against the law.”

She gently pulls down her top to reveal her left boob and twists her nipple gently between her thumb and index finger. “What about this officer? Is this against the law?”

“Ma'am please stop! Now that is indecent exposure.”

“Oh is it really officer? So men can have their shirts off in public but I can't? Isn't that called double standards?”

The officer pauses to carefully think about his answer.

Mary takes this opportunity and asks him, “Do you want to touch them officer?” Again the officer has nothing to say. “Go on. You know you want to Martinez,” she says while reading his name badge.

“You can call me Joe, Ma'am,” he responds.

“Oh I like that a lot better Joe.”

Joe looks around to see if there is anyone around then quickly grabs Mary's left boob.

“Oh my! Your hands are so strong. Do you like my tits Joe?”

He hesitates a little. “Yes ma'am. I do.”

“You can call me Mary.”

“Ok Mary. I don't want to get into trouble for this.”

“I promise I won't tell if you don't give me a ticket.”

He pulls out his hand from inside her car. “Ok but let's take this to the back of my cruiser.”

“Oh fuck yes...let's.”

Mary has never sat at the back of a police cruiser. This is exciting her in her twisted little mind. Joe opens the rear passenger door of the police cruiser and she sits inside. He looks around and then sits in next to her.

“What are you going to do to me Officer Joe? I know I've been a bad girl,” she says. She looks down at his crotch and can see a bulge. She puts her hand on his bulging dick, rubs it and says, “Oh my Officer Joe! You have a boner already. Let me see it.”

He obliges and unzips his pants.

She reaches inside and pulls out his cock. "Ooo I like your cock Officer Joe. It's so thick," she says. "Do you want me to suck it?"

He nods.

She leans over and licks the tip of his cock then puts it in her mouth. She moans as she sucks his dick. This is making her very wet. "Choke me with this big cock Joe," she says. "Fuck my throat."

He pumps his cock in her mouth, making her gag a little. Her throat makes a wet gagging sound as he pumps his cock in her mouth. Her saliva drools from the sides of her mouth all over his hard cock. She licks it all up and slurps it before pushing her face all the way down his hard cock. He gets really excited and even harder. His aggressiveness begins to show as he pushes her head forcefully on his hard throbbing cock and holds it there. She gags and her face and eyes start to turn red. She taps his leg signaling him that she can't breathe and he removes his hand from her head.

She sits up, gasps for air and strokes his cock with her hand. "You like that baby?"

"Yes I do."

"I want you to cum in my mouth Officer Joe," she says. "I wanna taste cop cum."

She leans over his crotch and puts his dick back in her mouth. She sucks it ferociously, gobbling it up balls deep. Her saliva covers the shaft of his dick which she is stroking as she sucks his cock head. She lifts up her head slightly. "Cum for me baby! Cum for me Officer Joe! Let me taste that cop cum. Give me every drop of it. I'm gonna swallow it all." She puts his hard throbbing cock back in her mouth and sucks it, moving her head up and down, up and down, up and down.

He starts to breathe loud. "Aaaahhh fuck I'm gonna cum," he shouts. "Aaaarrrrrgggghhhh! Aaaaaarrrrrrghhhh! Aaaarrrrghhhhh! I'm cumming."

She keeps sucking his dick up and down, up and down,

up and down with her lips tightly wrapped around his shaft making sure none of his cum escapes her mouth.

He shoots his big warm load of cum in her mouth and his body shakes. "Ohhh fuck baby yes! Take that cop cum! Take every drop of it! Swallow every drop of it!"

"Mmmmm…mmmmmm….mmmmmmm," she moans, as she swallows every last drop. She lifts her head and sighs in satisfaction as if her thirst was just quenched. She wipes her mouth with her hand. "Thanks for not giving me a speeding ticket Officer Joe."

9 LIT TRAIN

Ryan and Aaron have been planning a trip to New York for a while now but something always comes up and it doesn't happen. However, everything has come together and they have decided to take AMTRAK all the way from Houston to New York. They both have never taken the train cross-country so they both are very excited. It will be a long trip and they will get to see a bunch of states.

The day of their departure has arrived and Aaron's cousin has opted to drop them off at the train station. There doesn't seem to be a lot of travelers boarding the train at this stop and that's a good sign – the emptier the seats, the more room to move around the train.

They both are pleasantly surprised by the interior of the train. It almost looks like an airplane. These new trains have really come a long way from the old bus-looking interiors to the plush seats that resemble Business Class seats of a Boeing.

Their cabin is pretty vacant. Their tickets had them seated together but with all these vacant seats, they decide to pick and choose. Aaron finds him a seat he likes and Ryan looks around. There are maybe ten passengers in a thirty-seat cabin. Ryan is trying to look for any hot girls that might be traveling in the same cabin and so far he is disappointed. There are still 20 minutes until the train departs so there is still hope. He finds a seat he likes and settles down. It is a little dark so he cannot really see all the passengers but he can hear two girls talking to each other.

"That's a good sign," he thinks to himself.

The train is set to depart in 5 minutes and he decides to go to the smoking cabin for a smoke. Smoking is just one of those habits that bring people together in a strange lets-die-together kind of way. Ryan is not really a regular smoker but he uses the habit to socialize in bar patios by offering free smokes to anyone who wants them. This way he comes off as generous and doesn't have to smoke all 20 cigarettes by himself. And he thinks less poison for himself.

"This is cool," he thinks, as he looks around the smoking cabin.

This will definitely be a place that he can spend talking to strangers on this long train ride. He pulls out a cigarette and lights it up. There are all kinds of people in this cabin but he is only concerned with hot girls which he doesn't see even one of. It will be a long and lonely train ride if there are no attractive females to converse with. He finishes his cigarette halfway like he usually does and goes back to his seat.

"So did you see any hot chicks?" Aaron asks.

"No man. Not a single one," he replies.

"Oh well…don't worry. Maybe there are some in the next cabin over."

"Let's hope so dude otherwise it will be a boring train ride."

The train route they have chosen will go north first through Arkansas, Missouri and Illinois and then go east through Indianapolis, Ohio, Pennsylvania and then arrive at New York. They both will be visiting these states for the first time. They will not really be visiting but just passing through the middle of the states should be fun. There should be lots of scenic landscape to see along the route. The train's dining cabin offers large panoramic windows to really get a good look at the passing scenery while sipping on a cup of morning coffee.

The train finally departs and they both are settled in their seats. Within 20 minutes of the journey, they both doze off.

Ryan wakes up from his nap and realizes it's been an hour already. He decides to go for a smoke. As he walks into the cabin, he spots a young attractive girl sitting with a friend. They both have eye contact and he finds a vacant seat to sit across from her.

"Yes baby," he thinks to himself.

He smiles at her while having his smoke and she smiles back. He thinks he will have plenty of opportunities to speak to her so he doesn't approach her right now. He likes to take his time in deciding the right thing to say and really build some sexual tension before he approaches women. There has been plenty of eye contact so far between the two so he knows that there is mutual attraction. He finishes his smoke and walks back to his seat. The girl follows soon after and as she passes by his seat, they both smile at each other and say hi. She sits one row behind him on the opposite side.

He turns his head, points to the seat next to her and asks, "Is that seat taken?"

She responds, "No it's not."

"May I join you?"

She smiles. "Yeah sure…I wouldn't mind company. It's going to be a long ride."

"Hi I'm Ryan," he says while offering his hand for a shake.

"Hi Ryan, I'm Allie," she says while shaking his hand.

"Wow that's a firm handshake for a girl."

"Oh it's all in the first handshake," she replies while winking at him.

They both laugh.

He finds out that she is going to Arkansas which will arrive much earlier than his destination. So he thinks he better make the most of this encounter.

Ryan is an open book and doesn't like to hide anything from his friends. He sometimes tends to overshare and Aaron is always trying to shut him up. Ryan likes being transparent. It is a liberating feeling.

Aaron can see him talking to a girl and he keeps turning his head every now and then to look. Ryan catches his glimpse and winks at him. Aaron can easily eavesdrop on their conversation. In fact, Aaron has already given him the look that he is oversharing with this girl and it might backfire. But he doesn't care as long as he gets to spend time with this girl and maybe get to kiss her.

He finds out that Allie is going back home after being in Oregon for a while. She seems to be a very liberal-minded young girl. She has had a lot of life experience already at her young age. Ryan is always impressed with intelligent girls. He finds intellect very sexy in women. He already has great respect for women in general and thinks they are the most beautiful and strongest creatures on earth.

The conversation he is having with her is like foreplay for him. He has this warm, tingling sensation in his brain which he doesn't always experience with girls. He knows she's into him because of the way her eyes are alternating between his eyes and his lips. He really thinks he is getting somewhere with her. They decide to go have a smoke.

As they are walking back from the smoking cabin, he walks behind her to get a good look at her ass. She has a pretty decent one. He can't wait to grab it.

As they sit and continue their conversation, she shares with him that her stop is not too far away. This is the cue for him to make a move ASAP.

He looks at her and asks, "Can I kiss you Allie?"

She smiles. "Yes you may Ryan."

He leans in for the kill. They start making out

passionately. She's got a tongue ring which he loves. He plays with the barbell with the tip of his tongue. He sucks on her lower lip while his hands grab her tits from over her tank top and rubs them.

She gets on top of him while running her fingers through his hair and he grabs her round juicy ass from over her blue faded jeans. She starts grinding her crotch on his hard erection as they kiss.

He moves his lips to her neck and kisses, licks and sucks on it. She starts moaning. He slides his hands inside her pants from behind so he can touch her bare ass. Her ass cheeks feel so smooth and warm against his palms. That makes his cock even harder.

She slides her hand down the front of his pants and grabs his cock. She starts rubbing it and stroking it while they make out. They so want to fuck each other's brains out but they know they can't. It is just too risky. Luckily it is late at night and it's dark in this part of the cabin so no one can really notice what's happening.

She whispers in his ear as she strokes his hard cock inside his pants, "Let's go to the very back so I can jack you off."

They get up from their seats and walk to the back of the cabin. Aaron is fast asleep so Ryan doesn't have to deal with his judging eyes. They sit at the very back on the right side where it's even darker and vacant. She sits next to him and they start making out again. He slides his hand in her pants to feel her pussy and it is extremely warm and wet. She starts to moan as he rubs her pussy. She unbuttons her pants and unzips without taking her pants off so he can have easy access to her wet, warm, juicy young pussy. He does the same for her. She pulls out his hard cock, spits on her hand and starts stroking it. He can't believe he is getting a hand job on a train while rubbing a girl's pussy. This feels too good.

"Hold on. Let me grab my lotion bottle," she says.

She pours some lotion on her hand along with her spit

and this lube recipe feels amazing. He has never felt this sensation on his cock before. She strokes his cock and balls with this homemade lube and kisses his neck while he goes back to sliding his fingers up and down her clit and wet pussy lips. The thought of having public sex is really making them even hornier. She starts moaning as she is about to cum. She tries very hard to moan quietly as to not be noticed and muffles her moans by pressing her lips on his neck. Hearing her cum and the warm, soft, wet humming sensation against his neck drives him insane and he starts to moan as he comes closer to orgasm as well.

She feels his hard cock get harder as she notices he is close to cumming. She starts stroking his cock faster and whispers in his ear, "Cum baby! Let me feel your warm cum spurt out of your cock onto my hand."

Hearing her say that does it for him. He grabs her thigh and squeezes it as he plants his lips on hers to muffle his moans and starts to cum while his body shakes and quivers. He shoots his big warm load of cum all over her hand as she keeps stroking it till she squeezes the last drop from his mushroom cock head.

10 TURNT BEACH

It is a pleasant Friday night by the beach. The moon is bright and its light is reflecting in the gentle waves of the ocean. There are a lot of young and beautiful people walking on the pier, drinking in the bars and laughter can be heard all around you, mingled with the distant sound of music and the faint scent of the ocean.

Jessica has just finished work, has done all her chores for the day and is ready to go out, have a few drinks and just enjoy the night. She walks into her favorite bar on the pier looking ravishing in her little black dress with her sexy cleavage showing off her beautiful body. She orders her favorite drink and is just leaning against the bar when a handsome young man catches her eye. This young man is tall, lean and has a rugged all-American look about him. At that moment Jessica's eyes lock in gaze with the young sexy man and there is an invisible force of attraction that can be felt by the both of them. Jessica immediately and subconsciously starts twirling her long brown hair with her index finger and looking at the man in a shy but inviting manner. The young man cannot resist Jessica's charm and starts to walk towards her.

"Hi there, I'm Dave," says the young man to Jessica.

She responds and the communication begins. Dave asks her about how her night is going and what her plans are after the bar.

"Oh I'm just relaxing on this pleasant Friday night," she says.

They start flirting with each other and gently touching each other on the arms and hands showing interest and physical attraction. After finishing their drinks they decide to go for a walk on the beach.

The ambience of the beach is very romantic with the moonlight reflecting on the waves and the temperature just right and comfortable. Jessica and Dave by now have created a very comfortable rapport and have already decided in their minds that they will be sleeping with each other very soon. In fact, they are both hoping that they will fulfill their fantasy of having sex on a moonlit night at the beach. Dave reaches for Jessica's hand and she gladly lets him hold it. They come across a lifeguard tower and decide to walk up to its little porch.

They both look out at the moonlight reflecting on the ocean waves and Dave puts his arm around Jessica's waist. At that moment, she turns her head to face him and he leans in for the kiss. They start making out and touching each other's sexy bodies. He reaches for her tits and starts squeezing them over the shirt, while he kisses her luscious, soft, warm, juicy lips, gently biting on her lower lip. They play with each other's tongues while he reaches for her perfectly toned ass from under her short black dress and pleasantly finds her wearing a G-string. He grabs her ass cheeks and squeezes them while she reaches for his toned ass and gives it a good squeeze. She can feel his big erection rubbing against her crotch and her pussy is getting really wet. He pulls out her tits from her dress and starts sucking on her nipples while squeezing them. She starts to moan with pleasure. He then moves his right hand over to her already warm and wet pussy, rubs it from over her G-string, and slowly pulls the front of the G-string aside so he can feel her wet pussy with his fingers. He finds it to be extremely wet, warm, hairless and smooth. She slides her hand inside the front of his pants so she can hold his surprisingly big dick. She moans as she grabs and holds his big, thick, long, hard and throbbing cock in her hand and can feel the veins on the shaft of his penis.

She kneels down in front of him, unbuttons his pants and pulls out his big hard cock. She licks the tip of his big mushroom cock head and slowly puts it inside her warm, wet mouth. Her luscious and soft lips wrap around his beautiful dick as she tries to take it deep down her throat until she gags on it. He runs his fingers through her beautiful brown hair and holds it in a ponytail as she pushes her face on his big hard throbbing cock and sucks it as deep as she can while grabbing his balls in her hand and gently massaging them. She then holds his hard cock in her hand and starts licking his balls and gently sucking on them. At this point, they are both moaning with pleasure. She is getting dripping wet at this point and he is rock hard.

He pulls her up from her kneeling position, turns her around so she leans against the wooden wall of the lifeguard tower, pulls up her black dress to reveal her perfectly toned ass, and rubs his cock head on her extremely wet, warm and soft pussy lips. He slides the head of his dick in between her pussy lips before slowly inserting his big, thick, long and hard cock all the way inside her wet, warm pussy. She gasps as he goes balls deep inside her and feels herself being filled up. She starts moaning and breathing heavily as he starts to pump his big cock in and out, in and out, in and out, harder, faster and deeper with every stroke. Her perfectly juicy and round ass hits his pelvis and makes a slapping sound as he pounds her from behind. His right hand holds her right ass cheek while his left hand grabs her hair gently pulling on it, while he kisses her neck and sucks on her ear lobe. His hand then moves to her back as he slides it down from her neck all the way down to her lower back dimples. He then uses both his hands, grabs her bare tits, squeezes them and gently twists her nipples between his index fingers and thumbs, while still pounding her pussy hard, fast and deep. He then slows down his thrusts while he turns her head so he can kiss her luscious mouth and play with her tongue.

Jessica turns around and wants to take charge now. She tells Dave that she wants to ride him. So he lies down on the floor and she sucks his dick a little, making it harder, before climbing on top of him and slowly sliding his big, hard cock inside her dripping wet and warm pussy. She moans and then kisses his mouth while placing her hand on the side of his face and feels his strong jawline. He grabs both her ass cheeks with both his hands, squeezes them and helps her ride him by moving her round ass up and down, up and down, up and down his big hard throbbing cock.

He now wants her on her hands and knees so he can pound her doggy style. She gets on her hands and knees, turns her head to look at him, as he slides his big hard cock inside her wet, warm, soft pussy from behind. She gasps as he starts pumping really hard, fast and deep. She can feel his cock hitting her insides. She loves this position as his perfectly sized and shaped cock massages her G-spot. He loves the image of her perfectly toned round ass moving back and forth, back and forth, back and forth on his big, thick, long and hard cock. She can feel coming really close to having an orgasm, and at that point, he also starts moaning louder and starts thrusting faster. It seems like they are going to have a simultaneous orgasm. She exclaims that she is going to cum and he also shouts the same. His thrusting becomes really hard and fast and it is at this point that she moans really loudly and starts to orgasm, her whole body shaking and trembling with pleasure. Watching her cum makes him really excited and he can't control himself so he pulls out his cock and moans loud as he shoots his big, warm load of cum all over her bare ass.

11 DRIVE-THRU CRUNK

There is a long line at the drive-thru but Ed is about to get off from work so he doesn't mind serving the last few customers. The last car of his shift pulls up to the drive-thru window and he hands over the customer's order.

"Thank you…what's your name? Oh Ed…thank you Ed! It is always a pleasant experience when a young, respectful and handsome young man greets you at the drive-thru," she says to him after looking at his name badge while smiling flirtatiously.

"Thank you! I really appreciate the compliment," he replies with a grin on his face. "What is your name?"

"Oh you can call me Susan."

"Hi Susan, that's a nice car you have there."

"I'm glad you like it Ed. Wait till you see my house…that is if you would like to."

He pauses for a second before replying because he doesn't want to lose this opportunity that is being handed to him by the Universe in a silver platter. "Oh wow. I'm so flattered. That answer is a resounding yes. I would love to see your house."

She grabs her Chanel bag from the backseat of her Bentley, pulls out her business card and hands it over to him. "I'm only going to give this to you if you promise to text me."

He takes the card and reads her name. "I would be stupid to miss out on an opportunity of checking out the house of a porn star."

"Ex-porn star," she corrects him.

They both laugh, bid their farewells and she drives off.

Ed clocks out and walks to his car. He is really excited to have met an ex-porn star. He has actually seen a bunch of her videos on PornHub. She looks a little different now that she's older and that's why he couldn't recognize her right away. Nonetheless, she is still very sexy. He imagines that she must be in her late 40s now. He sits in his car and googles her name. She even has her own Wikipedia page. He was right, she is 46 now. He clicks on the Images tab and scrolls through some of her nude pictures. He starts getting hard. He thinks about texting her right now. He thinks it would be a good idea to strike the iron while it's hot. So he first saves her number as a contact in his phone and then texts her: "Hi Susan. This is Ed. We just met at the Jack in the box drive-thru. It was really nice meeting you. I hope this isn't too forward but I'm off of work and was wondering if you would like to meet tonight?" He starts to drive towards his house which is only a couple miles away.

He arrives home and gets in the shower. His phone buzzes while he is showering and he wonders if it is Susan who has replied to his text. He gets out and dries himself quickly. He picks up his phone in anticipation and finds out that it was a stupid marketing text from his local marijuana dispensary. He is a little disappointed. "But then again it has only been 30 minutes since I texted her. Maybe she is busy," he thinks. He goes back to drying himself off and gets dressed.

He scrolls through his Netflix app to find a good movie to watch while lying in bed. He finds a romantic comedy and decides to watch it. While watching the movie he picks up his phone to check his messages again but nothing from Susan. It is about an hour now since he texted her and he begins to think that she was just being nice. He is a little disappointed but he decides to counter that feeling by watching one of her porn videos on PornHub. He finds one, clicks on it and starts watching her getting fucked by two guys at the same time. One guy's fucking her mouth while the other guy's fucking her pussy doggy style while spanking her ass really hard. Ed starts to get an erection and decides to masturbate. He grabs the bottle of hand lotion on his desk starts to rub his dick and balls. Watching her getting fucked so hard and rough by these two guys is making him really rock hard. Now the two guys in the video are fucking her ass and pussy together. This view of double penetration is what gets him close to orgasm. He gets really close to ejaculation when suddenly there is a text from Susan. He reads the text while still stroking his cock and it reads "Hey sexy" and that is enough for him to make him cum instantly and ecstatically.

She explains to him that the reason for being late in her reply was that she was removing all her body hair before taking a bath and she had left her phone in her room. She also had a glass too many of her favorite wine so she lost track of time. He doesn't mind because better late than never. She wants to meet him tonight and gives him her address. He looks it up on Google Maps and taps on Street View so he can see what her house looks like. It has an amazing view of the harbor. He quickly dresses, gets in his car and starts driving to her house.

He arrives at her beautiful house, parks his car and walks up to her front door. She greets him in tight black yoga pants and a fluorescent pink tank top and invites him in. "Would you like a glass of wine?" she asks.

"Yeah sure!" he answers.

She leads him to her living room that has floor to ceiling windows overlooking her pool and a beautiful view of the harbor lights. "Should I light the fireplace?" she asks.

"Yes that would be nice," he replies.

It is a very romantic setting as they both sit on her L-shaped couch, sipping on wine with the warmth of the fireplace. Ed notices how the glow of the fireplace is illuminating her tan skin in a sensual tone of sexy. He starts imagining licking her soft smooth tan body. He starts getting a hard-on again and she notices.

"So Ed tell me about yourself. What do you like to do when you're not working?" she asks.

"I actually design websites as a hobby as well as for clients every now and then," he replies.

"Oh that's interesting. I actually might need help with my website. I am trying to set up a Patreon site for myself to sell my nudes. You think you can help me with that."

"Oh yes of course I can."

"Great! Maybe we can have a great business relationship."

"So is that all you're looking for? A business partnership?"

"Well what do you want Ed?"

"I would love for us to have a business/pleasure relationship."

"I'm open to that. I think we can work well together. On that note, do you smoke weed? Would you like to smoke with me?"

"I do occasionally actually."

"Let me grab my vape then," she says.

He waits for her on the couch, looking out at the beautiful view and sips on the wine. He pulls out his phone and decides to take a picture of the fireplace. She walks in at that moment and walks into the frame. "Hey you have to ask me before you take my picture," she says and they both laugh. They take a few puffs of the weed vape pen and he starts to feel it right away.

"Wow I'm really high already. Sorry I'm a lightweight

when it comes to weed and alcohol," he admits.

"No worries Ed. I'll be gentle with you," she says and touches his thigh.

He hasn't had sex in a couple months now and his boner is about to tear through his pants. At that moment, he spontaneously leans over and kisses her lips. She is surprised for a moment, but reciprocates. They kiss passionately while he grabs her tits from over her tank top. He feels her implants.

"No wonder they looked so damn good," he thinks. He squeezes them and feels her erect nipples poking through her tank top. He pulls her tank top off so he can access her beautiful round firm tits. He puts her erect nipple in his mouth and sucks on it with his warm, wet, soft tongue. She moans.

"Let's take this to my bedroom, shall we?" she says.

She already has scented candles burning in her room. It smells delicious and sensual. She has a big King-size bed with lots of pillows.

"Take your clothes off," she demands. He obliges. "Oh wow! That is a nice cock!" she exclaims as she sees his hard erection pop out as he pulls down his underwear. She immediately gets down on her knees in front of him, holds his hard cock in her hand and licks the tip of his cock head. He puts his hand gently on the back of her head as she takes his hard cock in her mouth. Her mouth feels so good. Her warm, wet lips wrap around his hard cock and she pushes her head all the way down his shaft till her lower lip touches his balls.

"Oh fuck that feels good!" he exclaims.

"Mmm-hmm," she mumbles with her mouth full of his big, thick, long and hard cock. She lifts his cock up till it touches his belly and starts licking his balls. She puts her warm, wet soft lips over his ball sack and gently sucks on his balls. She licks his ball sack all the way from the bottom to the tip of his cock head before putting his hard cock back in her mouth. She really starts to fuck her own mouth with his hard cock, pushing her head back and forth, back and forth, back and forth on his hard cock making a wet gagging sound. He loves the sound of her wet throat against his big hard cock. It makes him even harder.

"Fuck baby I can't wait for you to fuck me with that big cock of yours!" She stands up and pushes him on her bed.

He falls on the bed on his back. "Damn girl…I like that dominance. What a fuckin' turn-on!"

She gets on her hands and knees and sucks his hard cock deeper and more aggressively. Her saliva drips all over his hard cock and balls. She licks it all up with her tongue and covers his whole cock with it. The sight of his hard cock shining with all her spit is making him even bigger and harder. He holds her hair in a ponytail as she sucks his big, thick, long and hard cock and licks and sucks his big juicy balls.

"Fuck me!" she begs.

"Let me lick that wet pussy of yours first baby!" he says.

She rolls on her back and spread her legs open. He plants his lips on her wet pussy lips. She is extremely wet already. He licks her clit with the tip of his tongue and puts two fingers inside her pussy. She is really tight for a 46 year old. He moans as he licks her clit, letting his saliva drip all over her pussy. He slides his warm, wet soft tongue in between her pussy lips up and down, up and down, up and down, making her pussy even wetter with his spit and her pussy juices. She moans louder and holds his head over her pussy, running her fingers through his hair as she eats her pussy like he is starving. He slobbers all over her pussy, covering it with his whole mouth. "Oh fuck you eat pussy good baby!" she exclaims.

"I'm loving this fresh tight wet pussy. Fuck it's so wet and pink," he replies. He swirls the tip of his tongue over her clit up and down and in circles until she can't take it anymore.

"Oh fuck baby I'm gonna cum," she shouts. Her whole body convulses as she cums while he keeps licking her pussy. His hands squeeze her tits and nipples as she cums in his mouth.

"Fuck me baby. I want that big dick inside me," she moans.

He gets up, lifts her legs, spreads them wide open and rubs his hard cock on her wet warm pussy lips. He rubs his big mushroom cock head over her clit before he slowly slides it in her pussy.

"Oh fuck your pussy feels so fuckin' good baby," he says.

"It's all yours baby. Fuck that pussy!" she shouts.

He starts to pound her pussy hard and balls deep. He fills her pussy up with his big hard cock and his cockhead hits her insides as she gasps for air.

"Oh fuck baby you're so big!" she says.

"Yeah? You like that big dick inside you baby? Huh? You like that big hard cock pounding that fuckin' wet pussy?" he says.

"Yes baby. I love that big cock. Give it to me. Give every inch of that big hard cock to me. Fuck me baby. Fuck me harder!" she says.

He kisses her mouth, plays with her tongue with his tongue and gently sucks on her lower lip while his big, thick, long and hard cock pounds her tight, wet, warm and juicy pussy. His body slaps against her body as he fucks her hard, deep and fast. He fucks her fast then slows down his pace and sucks on her nipples. He squeezes and rubs her big tits and sucks on her nipples while his hard cock slides in and out of her wet pussy, making his cock shine with her juices in the candlelight.

"Fuck me doggy!" she says.

She gets up on her hands and knees, arches her back and sticks out her ass for him to fuck. He grabs her ass with both his hands, squeezes her ass cheeks and spanks them. He buries his face in between her ass cheeks and licks her pussy in doggy style. He smacks her juicy round ass cheeks one more time, before he pushes his hard cock back inside her wet warm juicy pussy. He starts pounding her deep.

"Fuck me Eddy! Fuck me baby! Fuck me hard! Yeah just like that!" she screams.

He holds her hair and pulls on it as his other hand holds her waist while pounding her pussy doggy style. Her jiggling ass cheeks slap against his thighs and pelvis and he fucks her deep and hard. He thrusts his big, thick, long hard cock in and out, in and out, in and out, deeper, faster and harder with every stroke.

"Oh fuck baby I'm gonna cum!" she screams. "Oh fuck I'm cumming. I'm cumming. I'm cumming!" she screams louder. She cums all over his hard cock while he keeps thrusting her pussy with his big cock. Her whole body shakes and shivers as she cums.

He spits on her ass hole, rubs it with his thumb and slowly slides it in.

"Fuck my ass baby," she says to him upon feeling his thumb inside her.

He pulls out his cock from her pussy and slowly inserts it in her ass.

"Oh fuck yes. Fuck that ass!" she shouts.

He pushes his cock in deeper in her ass.

"Fuck baby your ass is tight!" he exclaims.

"Yeah? You like that ass hole wrapped around your hard cock? It's yours baby. Fuck my ass. Make it yours!"

He pulls her hair as he starts to fuck her ass deeper and faster. The thought of fucking an ex-porn star's ass makes him feel like one of those guys he watched in her porn video. The sight of his hard cock sliding in and out of her ass hole is making him extremely horny and he is just about to cum.

"Baby I'm gonna cum!" he shouts.

"Cum in my mouth baby! I wanna drink every drop of

that cum!" she moans.

He pulls out his cock, she turns around and puts his cock in her mouth. She sucks on it for a minute until he shouts, "Fuck I'm gonna cum!"

"Cum baby! Give me that big load of hot cum in my mouth!"

"Ohhh fuck baby! Aaaaaahhhh! Arrrggghhhh! Fuck! Aaaaaaaaaaaarrrrrrgggghhhh!" he shouts as he cums inside her mouth. Her lips are still wrapped around his cockhead as he shoots his big load of warm cum inside her mouth.

"Mmmm! Mmmm! MMMMM!" she moans while drinking his cum. She looks into his eyes and swallows every drop of his cum. "Wow that was a lot of cum! Good protein for my hair!"

"I'm glad to be of service Madame!" he replies and they both laugh together lying on their backs.

12 STRAIGHT FIRE DELIVERY

It's the end of a very long day for Alyssa and she is ready to go home to a hot relaxing bath. Alyssa works at the local gym as a personal trainer. When she isn't helping clients with their workout regimens or consulting with them about their meal plans, she is busy working away on her computer at her desk. She loves her job. One of the perks of her jobs is that she gets to see fit muscular men lift weights in front of her. Sometimes it is overwhelming for her because she has been single for a few months now and has been really horny lately. Sometimes, as she is typing away a meal plan for a client, she glances at a hot muscular guy working on his back or doing leg workouts and starts to drift away into a day dream of having sex with him on one of the gym machines. She starts to get really aroused as she is fantasizing and starts chewing away at her ball point pen. While she is chewing away, she suddenly realizes she must not get distracted and focus on the job at hand. You can see a pen holder at her desk with about ten pens whose caps have been bitten to shreds.

The clock strikes 6 and Alyssa grabs her duffle bag, says her farewells to her colleagues and heads out the door. While she is driving back home, she is thinking about what she wants to have for dinner. It's the weekend for Alyssa and she doesn't feel like cooking at all tonight. So she decides to order something from the Door Dash app. She loves the Door Dash food delivery app and uses it on the weekends when she feels lazy and wants to treat herself. She deserves to spend the little extra on dinner tonight since she has had a really tough week. It has been really exhausting. She feels like ordering some spicy Thai food tonight. At the next red light, she quickly swipes through her favorite Thai restaurants in her neighborhood and finds one she likes. She orders her favorite Thai dish and is notified that it will be delivered in 45 minutes. Perfect! It gives her just the right amount of time to get back to her apartment and prepare a hot bath for herself.

She reaches home, throws her duffle bag on the floor, takes off her clothes, wears her lush bath robe and prepares her bath. She sets the mood by lighting a few scented candles and places them around the bath tub. She looks at the clock and there is still 30 minutes left until her food arrives. So she decides to jump in the bath with a glass of merlot. The bath feels so amazing. She works out at her gym on her lunch break every other day and today she worked on her legs and back. Her muscles are a little sore but they have already started to heal against the hot relaxing bath water. She puts on her Spotify playlist and closes her eyes as she lays her head at the edge of the tub.

There is a knock on her door and she wakes up realizing she had drifted away into a relaxing nap. That half an hour in the bath and that wine has really gotten her into a good mood. She grabs her bath robe, puts it on and heads to her door. She looks through the peephole and it surely is her Thai food. She opens the door and is very pleasantly surprised by how handsome this Door Dash delivery guy is.

"Hi Alyssa?" asks the delivery guy.

"Yes that would be me," replies Alyssa with the biggest smile on her face.

The delivery guy is tall, dark and handsome, just the way Alyssa likes her men and he can't keep his eyes off of her silky, smooth, toned legs that are peaking through the side of her robe as she grabs the bag of food from his hand.

"Thank you so much! I am starving!" she exclaims.

The delivery guy smiles and says, "You're most welcome Alyssa."

She awkwardly reaches out with her hand to shake his.

He is taken aback since customers usually don't do that. But he obliges and shakes her hand back.

She gives his hand a good squeeze as that is the only physical contact she has received from a man in over two months. She quickly realizes that she might be creeping the guy out, releases his hand and says, "I'm sorry."

The guy replies, "Oh no of course not…don't be sorry. Have a goodnight!" And he walks away.

She closes her door and is so extremely horny at this point. She curses herself for not taking the perfect opportunity of asking him to come inside. But then realizes how stupid that move would be. He is a complete stranger. But all delivery personnel at Door Dash go through a background check just like Uber and Lyft drivers do, she rationalizes.

"Oh well it's too late now Alyssa…you could have gotten some kind of action but you blew it," she thinks. As she steps away from the door and puts her food on her dinner table, she hears a knock on the door. "Who could this be?" she whispers. She peeps through the peephole and sees the delivery guy holding up a plastic bag.

So she opens the door and the guy says, "I'm sorry to bother you but I forgot to give you your salad."

She smiles and thinks, "This is your chance Alyssa. Take it!" She says, "Thanks! Uh…so I was wondering…uh…would you like to come in for a drink?" She regrets it as soon as she asks that question, cringing inside with a big dorky grin on her face.

"Uh…umm…ok sure. Thanks!"

She closes the door behind them, turns to him and extends her hand again. "Hi I'm Alyssa."

He shakes her hand. "Hi Alyssa. Nice to meet you…I'm Sameer."

"Oh that's an interesting name. Where are you from?"

"I'm Middle Eastern,"

"Oh nice! I love Middle Eastern food!" she responds and they both start laughing. "Please take a seat."

They both sit at the dinner table.

"I'm sorry I'm not dressed for the occasion," she apologizes as she adjusts the belt of her robe.

"Oh neither am I," replies Sameer. They both laugh.

"Would you like a glass of wine or beer?"

"I'll drink whatever you are drinking."

She walks to her kitchen and admits, "I'm sorry I never do this. I'm really nervous."

"Neither do I! I have never had a customer invite me inside their home."

She walks back with a glass of wine for him and hands it over. "Well there is a first for everything right?"

"There surely is."

They both go about sharing their life stories while sipping on the wine. The food just sits there in the middle of the table, untouched. Sameer realizes he has just drunk the whole glass of wine within 15 minutes. Alyssa looks at the glass. "Would you like another one?"

"Sure!"

She brings him another glass of wine. "Would you like to sit on the couch and watch a movie maybe?"

"Sure"

They take the party to the couch.

She notices Sameer's butt as he walks to the couch and can't wait to grab it. "He looks too fit and good looking to be straight," she thinks. "Maybe he is gay and that's why he hasn't flirted with me yet." She sits next to him on the couch. She makes it a point to expose her sexy, smooth, bare thigh from under her bath robe slit as she flips through the movie selection on Netflix, hoping he will get enticed into making a move on her. She asks him which movie he would like to see. He says he doesn't care. He does notice how toned her thigh is and is starting to get hard in his pants. She notices the bulge in his pants from her peripheral vision and gets a little wet. She tries to pass the remote to him, "Do you want to decide on the movie?" and purposely drops the remote on his bulge.

The remote lands directly on his hard erection and he exclaims, "Oops!"

They look at each other, start laughing. He picks up the remote, puts it aside and reaches for her thigh. She sees his attempt and leans in towards him and plants her lips on his. Game is ON!

They both kiss passionately, while he sucks on her luscious lower lip and gently nibbles on it, while sliding his hand under her robe to squeeze her soft, big tits. He gently rubs her erect nipples between his thumb and index finger while playing with her tongue and sucking on it. They both start moaning.

She rubs his hard cock from over his pants and then unbuttons them. She pulls out his hard cock and is pleasantly surprised by his big cock. She starts stroking it while he kisses and licks her neck and sucks on her ear lobe.

He then moves down to her tits and licks her nipples with his soft, warm and wet tongue. She moans. He puts her soft erect nipples in his mouth and sucks on her nipples, using the tip of his tongue to flick her nipples. He then licks her areolas and moves his tongue in circles around her nipples, squeezing her tits at the same time. He licks and sucks her left boob, while squeezing and rubbing her right one. He kisses, licks and sucks every inch of her left boob and then moves to her right one.

She is moaning and stroking his hard cock and balls and has become extremely wet.

As he sucks her right boob, he pulls off her robe and slides his hand from her boobs to her stomach. He feels her belly ring and is impressed by how flat and toned her stomach is. He slides his hand further down between her legs and she spreads her legs open. He touches her shaved and extremely warm and wet pussy. She is dripping wet at this point. He slides his fingers in between her pussy lips and rubs her clit with his thumb. He then licks his fingers to taste her pussy juices. He kneels down in front of her while she spreads her legs wide open for him to have full access to her pretty wet pussy. He starts kissing her feet and moves his lips over her calves, alternating between her legs, as he kisses all the way down to her thighs. He kisses, licks and gently bites her inner thighs, as he slides his soft, wet and warm lips over to her extremely wet and juicy pussy. He slides his wet, warm and soft tongue in between her pussy lips, sticks his tongue inside her pussy and fucks her with his tongue. Her moans become louder and more intense. He then slides the tip of his tongue over to her clit and swirls it up and down and in circles, gently flicking her clit with his tongue. Her body starts to quiver and shake as she cums. He keeps licking her pussy and clit, as she places a hand over the back of his head and gently pushes his head on her pussy as if to fuck his mouth. He licks her pussy and clit a little faster as he notices her body start to shake and quiver again. He keeps swirling the tip of his tongue over her clit and start to feel it becoming erect and bigger.

Within seconds, she moans, "I'm cumming again. Oh my God Sameer! Just like that. Keep eating my pussy like that! Oh please don't stop!" She shakes and cums again.

He keeps eating her pussy for about 20 minutes and makes her cum 5 times.

"I want to suck that big hard cock of yours Sameer. Fuck my mouth!" she says.

He stands up in front of her while she sits on the couch and she holds his hard cock by the base of his shaft and licks his cock head. She then puts his engorged and rock hard cock in her mouth and sucks on it, making slurping sounds with her mouth. She drools all over his hard cock, her saliva dripping out of her mouth. She then holds his hard wet cock, lifts it up so she can suck his big balls. She licks and sucks his balls with her wet, warm, soft luscious lips and slides her tongue all over his ball sack making it all shiny wet with her spit. He is extremely hard. He holds her hair in a ponytail and pushes his hard cock deeper down her throat and fucks her pretty face with his big, thick, long and hard cock. She gags on his hard cock a little. But he keeps pumping his hard cock in her mouth as her mouth makes wet sloppy sounds. She hasn't sucked such a big cock before and is loving his hard cock in her mouth. He pushes his hard cock even deeper down her throat and pulls it all the way out.

"Stick your tongue out," he says. She does just that and he taps his cock head on her tongue before putting it back in her mouth.

She then gets on top of him, grabs his hard cock and starts to rub his cock head on her dripping wet, warm pussy and clit before guiding it inside of her. She kisses his mouth, grabs his hand and puts it on her juicy tits. He uses his other hand and grabs her ass cheek as she rides his hard cock up and down, up and down, increasing her pace of bouncing on his cock. They both start to moan louder with ecstasy. He sucks on her nipples, gently nibbling on them as he holds both her ass cheeks in his hands, squeezes them as she rides him like a wild cowgirl. Her ass slaps against his thighs as he fucks her hard, balls deep. Her pussy juices drip all over his hard cock and balls.

She gets off and starts to lick her juices off his hard cock and balls. "Mmm I taste so good on your cock," she exclaims. "Fuck me doggy baby."

He obliges, stands up and gets behind her as she leans on the top of the couch and sticks her ass out for him. He slaps her juicy ass, rubs his big mushroom cockhead on her wet pussy lips before inserting his big, thick, long and hard cock deep inside her. She feels him hit her insides and gasps for air as he starts pounding her harder, faster and deeper with every stroke. He holds her hair and pulls on it as he fucks her doggy style.

"Oh my God baby I'm gonna cum!" she shouts. Her pussy clinches on his hard shaft as her whole body quivers and she orgasms. "Ahhh baby yes. Fuck me harder!"

He pounds her pussy harder and harder while he grabs her ass cheeks and spreads them open. He spits on her ass hole and rubs it with his thumb and she loves it.

"Fuck my ass baby!" she says.

This really excites him since he hasn't done anal before.

"Go slow," she says.

He pulls his cock out from her pussy, spits on her ass hole again and slowly inserts his cock head.

"Oh fuck yes! Fuck my ass baby! Fuck it!" she moans.

He slowly inserts all of his hard cock inside her ass and slowly slides it in and out, in and out, increasing his pace with every thrust.

"Ah fuck baby your ass is so tight. Feels so good on my cock!" he tells her.

She starts to cum again as she rubs her pussy and clit with her hand while he fucks her ass deep.

"Lie down on your stomach," he says.

She spreads across the couch on her stomach. He climbs on top of her and slides his hard cock in her ass. He kisses her neck and shoulders as he fucks her.

"Oh fuck your cock feels so good in my ass," she says.

He fucks her in and out, in and out, deeper, faster with every stroke and she cums again.

"Oh fuck baby I'm cumming," she screams. "Aaahhh fuck yeah baby…fuck that ass…make me your slut!" she shouts.

He fucks her harder and harder. His breathing intensifies. He is about to cum as well.

He pulls out his cock from her ass and says, "Suck my

cock baby."

He sits back on the couch and she gets down on her knees in front of him. She spits on his hard cock and strokes it before putting it in her mouth. She deepthroats his cock until she gags. "Choke on this big cock!" he shouts.

She sucks his cock deeper, then pulls it out and sucks on his balls. She puts it back in her mouth and starts sucking harder while rubbing his balls.

"Fuck I'm gonna cum baby!" he shouts.

"Cum on my face baby!" she moans.

"Aaahhhhh fuck. Aaaaargh! Fuck baby I'm gonna cum," he shouts. His body starts to shake and he pulls her head off of his cock and stands up in front of her.

She looks up at him, opens her mouth and sticks her tongue out. He strokes his hard cock and starts to cum. "Aaahhhhh…aaahhhh….aaaahhhh!" he shouts as he shoots his big warm load of cum all over her pretty face and mouth.

She sucks his cock head and squeezes it with her hand to get every last drop of cum, then looks up at him and swallows it all.

13 GUCCI GIFT

Brothers Kyle and Seth have been going to the bars on the pier ever since they turned legal drinking age. And ever since their childhood friend Roger moved here, they go out twice, sometimes thrice a week. This trio has had a lot of experiences and met a lot of interesting people while partying at these beach bars. Sometimes they even come by themselves when the trio is incomplete. All the bartenders, waitresses and bouncers know them by name now. Each one of them has a story to tell.

Kyle is the eldest of the three and is the more dominant extrovert type. He's the guy you see at the bar trying to impress the girls with all kinds of untruths. He is usually embarrassing Seth and Roger when he socializes due to his elaborate stories, some true and some not so. He always says that you've got to tell people what they want to hear. And if little white lies will get him laid, then why not? Seth and Roger don't really believe in the same pickup techniques as Kyle does. But that doesn't stop their camaraderie. They all believe that there is a certain energy around them when the trio gets together and goes out. They feel they attract people towards them naturally without having to try too hard.

As usual on a Wednesday night, they walk up to the bouncer at their favorite bar and are greeted in. The bar is surprisingly packed today. There is a live band playing and there seems to be a lot of single ladies in the joint. The trio is excited and ready for the night.

Seth orders them all drinks, like he usually does as he is the one with the best paying job right now and he doesn't mind treating his brother and best friend whenever they go out. They decide to chill at the bar for a bit and watch the band play in front of them. Kyle decides to go socialize at the patio and have a smoke while Seth and Roger stay at the bar. They both have to keep an eye out for Kyle because he tends to get into fights and sometimes they get thrown out of the bar because of him. But Kyle seems to be in a good mood tonight so they aren't too worried about him.

After finishing their first drinks, Seth orders another round and they join Kyle in the patio. As usual Kyle is surrounded by a group of people who are listening attentively to whatever story he has chosen to tell tonight. Seth and Roger actually admire this quality about him especially since they both are introverts. So they join the group of people to listen in on the story. After a few minutes, Seth and Roger realize it is just another one of Kyle's stories about how he lost a cop car hot on his trail once with his amazing driving abilities. They give each other the yeah-right look and start looking around.

After trying to talk to some girls and getting nowhere, the three men decide to bar hop.

As they are walking out, Roger says to Seth, "Dude did you check out that blonde girl?"

Seth replies, "Which blonde girl?"

"Are you kidding me? She was checking you out like crazy man. You gotta go talk to her," Roger replies.

"But I don't even know who you are talking about," Seth replies. They all stop and turn around to take a look at this girl Roger is talking about.

"It is that one with the khaki pants," Roger points out.

Seth finds her in the crowd and she certainly is looking at him. "How could I not notice that she was checking me out?" he exclaims. "She is pretty hot."

"I'm telling you dude, from the way she was looking at you inside the bar, I bet you she will do anything for you man! Trust me…you gotta go talk to her," Roger says.

So Seth decides to go back inside the bar to see what this is all about.

As soon as he approaches the girl, she pulls out a napkin and a pen and starts writing on it. Seth at this point is pretty inebriated so this is kind of interesting. When he reads the napkin, he realizes that this girl is deaf. He has never been with a deaf girl before so he just plays along with it.

"I have been noticing you for a few days now. I saw you a few times at the pier and really wanted you to come talk to me. I'm so glad that you finally did," he reads what she has written on the napkin. She hands the pen over to him for him to write a reply.

"I had no idea…I'm sorry. If I had known you were checking me out, I would have definitely come over to talk to you," he writes.

"My name is Penny. What's your name?" she writes.

"I'm Seth," he writes back and then shakes her hand.

"I don't want to keep you too long since I know your friends are waiting for you outside, but I would love to see you same place same time tomorrow if that's not too much to ask," she writes.

"Wow this chick is really into me," Seth thinks and writes, "Oh yes of course. I would love to meet you again tomorrow." They hug each other and Seth walks out and joins his brother and friend.

"What happened? What were you guys writing about on the napkin?" Roger asks.

"Oh she is deaf man," Seth replies.

"No way!" Kyle laughs.

"Hey man don't be such a jerk! So what if she is deaf?" Seth exclaims.

"Hey I'm just wondering what she sounds like when she moans," Kyle says while smiling at Roger.

Seth hits his brother on his arm.

Kyle rubs his arm. "Ouch! Dude that hurt."

"I don't care what she sounds like when she moans because she is hot," Seth replies.

Kyle turns around to give her another look. "She certainly is dude. So anyway genius, did you get her number? Oh wait…how will you guys talk on the phone?"

"Oh damn I hadn't thought of that," Seth says.

"Haven't you heard of TTY man?" Roger cuts in.

"What is TTY?" Kyle asks.

"Oh yeah maybe she has one of those text telephones. It is a device where you can type what you want the operator to tell the person you are calling. And they basically just read out to you what the deaf person has typed into the device," Seth says.

"That is interesting! Yeah maybe she does have one of those," Roger replies.

"Well I didn't get her number but I'll just come here tomorrow at the same time as she will be here," Seth says.

"Well good luck dude. I hope she is," Kyle replies.

The trio decides to get something to eat and then head back home.

That night Seth lies in his bed and wonders what it would be like dating a deaf girl. He has been single for a while and any kind of female attention for him is welcomed. He is excited in a way. He is all about new experiences and is very open-minded. He has a positive feeling about the whole experience.

The next day Seth is on time at the bar where he met Penny last night. He grabs a drink at the bar and looks around but doesn't see her. So he decides to go out to the patio. He looks around and she is nowhere to be seen. He is a little disappointed and just goes to the corner table and sits down. There are lots of other gorgeous ladies at the bar but he just cannot seem to get the thought of Penny out of his mind. He was actually looking forward to seeing her tonight. "Oh well…at least I tried," he thinks to himself.

"Hi Seth," he hears and turns around and sees the waitress.

"Oh hi Jennifer!" he replies and gives her a hug.

"Are you waiting for someone?" she asks.

He looks at his watch. "Yeah I was supposed to see this girl I met last night. But she isn't here."

"Oh that's too bad. But give it some time. You've only been here for 10 minutes. She might be running late. Have you tried calling her?"

"Unfortunately I can't call her because for one I don't have her number and secondly, she is deaf."

"Ah ok. Well good luck to you Seth," she says while grabbing an empty beer bottle from a table.

"Yeah thanks!" He takes a seat at the corner of the patio.

He waits for another ten minutes and then decides to leave the bar. As he is about to walk out, he feels a tap on his shoulder. He turns around and it is Penny. They both smile at each other and hug. They both seem pretty happy to see each other. He knows he is for sure. They find a table and she pulls out a notebook and pen.

She starts writing, "I'm so glad you came and I'm sorry I'm late."

"It's ok…it was only 20 minutes."

"I forgot to give you my TTY number. Do you know what that is?"

"Yes I do know what that is. I was also regretting not getting your number last night."

"I actually also have Snapchat. You can even snap me on there."

"Oh that would be great. What is your username?"

They both exchange their usernames and then she

writes, "Do you want to get out of here? We can go on a walk to the beach if you'd like."

It is a nice night and he writes back, "Yeah sure." They both walk out the bar towards the beach.

It is a moonlit night and its reflection on the ocean waves looks textbook romantic. It is hard to write and walk at the same time so they just decide to walk quietly along the shore looking at the moon and then looking at each other and smiling every once a while. They come to a bench and decide to sit down.

She pulls out her notebook from her bag and writes, "I know I have told you this last night but I really wanted to talk to you for a while now. I've seen you a few times at the bars here and I'm so happy you came and talked to me."

"I'm really glad I did too."

"I actually live in that hostel next to the bar. Would you like to see my place?"

He gets excited and writes, "Yes very much so." And they walk to the hostel building and up to her room.

He has never been inside a hostel before. It looks like a smaller version of a college dorm. She shows him to her room. It is a small room with 4 bunk beds. He wonders what they could even do in a room that has no privacy. She points out that the upper bed is hers. They both climb on it. "Sorry that it's a small room and there is no privacy."

"It's ok."

"None of my roommates will be back until later tonight though."

He signals approval with a thumbs-up.

"I have a gift for you," she writes.

"Oh ok what is it?"

She puts the notebook aside, gets off from her bed on to the floor and he follows. She starts to rub his crotch and that gives him an instant erection. She looks him in the eyes and smiles. He leans over and kisses her. He gets harder as she unbuttons his pants and pulls them down.

He has somewhat of an idea what this gift is all about. His hard cock is poking out of his boxers. She kneels down in front of him and puts her face in his crotch over the boxers. She sniffs his cock and balls from over the boxers.

"This is interesting," he thinks. No girl has ever sniffed his crotch before.

She finally pulls down his boxers and out comes his hard cock like a horizontal flag pole. Her eyebrows go up in amazement. She signs with her hand that it's big. He smiles. She holds his cock and licks the tip of his cock head with her tongue and then puts his mushroom cockhead in her mouth. She sucks on it like a lollipop. She then pushes her mouth all the way down his cock shaft till every inch of his cock is down her throat.

"Woah! That is some gift! She is certainly gifted!" he thinks.

She makes a wet gagging sound with her throat as she tries to fuck her own face with his hard throbbing cock, *"gluk...gluk...gluk."* He gets rock hard. She pulls his cock out of her mouth and lifts it up so she can suck on his balls. She licks and sucks his ball sack all over with her soft, wet, warm mouth all the while sniffing it. She has some kind of fetish for the musky smell of balls. She then puts his hard throbbing cock back in her mouth. She sucks on it balls deep, pushing her face back and forth, back and forth, back and forth on his big hard cock. She pulls it out and slides her slightly open mouth and lips on the side of his cock shaft.

He is loving this amazing professional blowjob he is randomly getting from a girl he just met last night. He is in heaven at this point.

She keeps fucking her face with his big, throbbing, hard cock.

He is about to shoot his big load of cum but he wants to control his ejaculation, so he pulls out his cock and signals to her that he needs to wait. She understands and smiles.

He closes his eyes and takes a few deep breaths. When he thinks he can go again, he puts his hard cock back in her mouth and starts pumping it in and out, in and out, in and out while holding her head. She lets him fuck her face any way he wants. He pulls out his cock and she sticks her tongue out. He slaps his cock head on her wet, warm tongue. He turns her head sideways and pushes his cock to make her cheeks bulge with the shape of his cock head.

She moans as he fucks her mouth with his cock. He starts pumping harder, faster and deeper, shoving his hard cock deep in her throat. He gets close to ejaculation and starts moaning. He pumps his cock balls deep in her wet, warm mouth a few more times and takes his hands off her head so she can decide if she wants to let him cum inside her mouth or not.

She can feel his hard cock get really hard and can feel his engorged veins on his cock shaft and knows he is about to cum. She keeps sucking his cock and looks up at him to see his expressions of ecstasy. She is ready for his load of cum in her mouth. His jaw drops and he starts to shoot his big warm load of cum in her mouth. She keeps her soft, warm, wet lips wrapped around his cock as he shoots his warm cum in her mouth. He moans and cums every last drop in her mouth.

She raises her eyebrows and looks at him to signal how big the load is. She gulps down the big load of warm cum and sucks his cock head to make sure she gets every last drop. She looks up at him and sighs as if her thirst just got quenched. She gets up and gives him a quick peck on his lips before stepping out to go to the bathroom in the hallway.

He gets dressed and writes in her notebook, "Thank you for the amazing gift. I loved it!"

14 SUBWAY RATCHET

Sam takes the subway every day to work. He hops on at Union station going south, transfers to the westbound and then eventually gets off at Spadina. Every time he gets on the westbound train, he wishes he would see that one hot brunette who is always wearing these sexy business suits or other such business attire. She is tall, maybe 5' 8" and has an amazing body. She has straight dark brown hair that she sometimes puts up in a bun with some stray ends of locks loosely dangling from the bun like tiny knives. She has brown eyes and has fair skin but not pale. She seems to be a Latina or could even be Greek. Sometimes when Sam is sitting down on the subway seat, he would see her hop on at St. George and by that time the subway car is pretty full so she has no choice but to stand. She holds on to the pole in the middle and he watches her sexy, shapely side profile. She has such a nice round juicy ass. It's not too big, not too small…just right! Oh how he wishes he could grab that hot ass!

He loves to take the subway because he not only gets lucky sometimes and sees that Greek Goddess but just generally enjoys people-watching. People from all walks of life and backgrounds take the subway every day.

He pans the subway car and is hoping to see another hot girl or woman. He is disappointed and looks down on his phone. At the next stop, a lot more passengers hop on and the subway car is suddenly jam-packed. While he is flipping through his phone screen, he notices a pair of black women's heels right in front of his shoes. So he looks up and sees THE BRUNETTE standing right in front of him with her shoes close enough to touch his shoes. He is suddenly flustered as he locks gaze with the woman of his fantasy and is dumbfounded. He quickly looks away and starts playing with his phone again. He can feel her looking at him with his head down. So he musters up the courage to look up and smile at her. She smiles back.

This will be a 30 minute train ride and he better think of something to say or do before her stop arrives and she gets off, not knowing when he will see her again, if ever. But he just doesn't know what to say or do. He knows her stop is coming up pretty quickly. He is trying to think and think but alas. No witty openers come to mind.

The automated voice on the speaker says out loud: "Next stop Lawrence."

This is it. This is her stop. She puts her hand in her purse, getting ready to step out and the train comes to a stop. He looks at her one more time and gives her a half-ass smile and she turns around and walks out the subway car. He feels like such a pussy. But in that instance, his heart starts racing madly and he decides to get off at this stop even though his stop is still 10 minutes away. He sees the back of her head in the see of heads as she walks to whatever her job is.

He runs, catches up to her, comes up right beside her and says, "Hi." That's all he had to say to begin with.

She looks at him and says, "Hey."

Sam explains to her that he has seen her a few times and thought she was really hot. She giggles with flattery and they strike up a friendly conversation. Next thing you know he is walking her to her workplace.

Her name is Jenny. They have great chemistry and are smiling and laughing together already. Jenny tells him that they have arrived at her office building and he asks her for her phone number.

She smiles. "Well Sam how about this. How about we meet each other after work and I will give you my number then…deal?"

"Ok sure that sounds like a plan," he agrees.

They decide to meet at a bar on the corner of Lawrence and Euclid at 5:30pm.

Both Sam and Jenny keep thinking about each other as they go about their day, often catching themselves daydreaming about the limitless possibilities of this chance encounter. They are both looking anxiously at the clocks on their phones, their computer screens, the clocks on the walls and their watches throughout their day. The mixture of emotions they both are feeling is intoxicating. This cocktail of anxiety, uncertainty, spontaneity, adventure and lust is just the right mix to make them start fantasizing about all kinds of sexual acts with each other. The clock strikes 5:30pm and they both rush out of their work like it's an emergency.

He walks into the bar and sees her sitting at a table in a dark corner. Luckily the bar is not that busy and there is opportunity to really talk to each other. He gets themselves drinks and the flirting begins. They can't take their eyes off of each other. He asks if he can sit next to her on the bench seat. She smiles with approval. They talk and flirt and drink. He reaches for her thigh over her sexy pin-striped formal pants. He immediately gets a hard on. She very boldly reaches over to the bulge in his pants and is pleasantly surprised with the size and girth. They are both very turned on at this point. She unzips his pants from under the table so no one can see and slides her hand inside the opening of his boxers. She starts to rub his big hard throbbing cock in her soft freshly manicured hands.

The excitement of being in public is exhilarating. He reciprocates and slides his hand down her pants and inside her panties to reveal an extremely wet and bald pussy. He cannot wait to fuck the shit out of "Jenny from the train." They both give each other this look and know exactly what each other are thinking. He zips up, gets up and starts walking to the restroom. She follows shortly thereafter. They look around so no one is looking and both go into the women's restroom.

He has never been inside a woman's restroom. For a good minute, he pans the room and smiles. "Women's restrooms are so much nicer than men's restrooms," he thinks to himself.

Jenny holds his hand and walks him into one of the stalls. She unzips his pants, kneels down, pulls out his big thick long and hard cock and licks the tip of his cockhead. She then puts his cock in his mouth all the way down her throat. She has no gag reflex. She starts to deepthroat his cock back and forth, back and forth.

He holds her bun and guides her head over his hard cock. Her soft, warm, wet mouth and those juicy lips wrapped around his shaft feel like heaven. He starts moving his hips back and forth and starts to really fuck her face. Luckily no one else is in the restroom because you can hear the sound of a throat getting fucked pretty good. She holds his big juicy balls in both her hands and he pumps his big hard cock in her mouth and throat.

He is now rock hard and can punch a hole in the wall with his cock. He helps her up, kisses her mouth passionately while unbuttoning her dress shirt to reveal a sexy black lace bra. He loves black lace. It looks so sexy against her tan skin. He pulls out her perfectly sized tits and starts to suck on her nipples. They are already erect with arousal. He swirls his soft, warm, wet tongue around the areolas and flicks his tongue over her erect nipples. He then gently nibbles on the nipples and she squirms with arousal. He reaches for her pants, unbuttons them and they fall to the floor. He turns her around while she leans against the wall, gets down on his knees and slowly pulls down her sexy black lace panties. "Oh my God, what a sexy hot fuckin' ass you got."

She laughs. He kisses her bare ass cheeks, squeezes them, slaps them and then pulls them open to reveal her pussy lips and ass hole. She arches her back and her ass protrudes out, begging him to lick her pussy and ass. He obliges and starts to slide his warm, wet, soft tongue in between her wet, warm, juicy pussy lips. She moans with ecstasy. He spread her ass cheeks and digs his tongue in her delicious wet pussy and licks her clit with the tip of his tongue. He then proceeds to finger her while he eats her pussy. He then slides his tongue over her perfect and clean ass hole and licks it.

She moans. "Oh God baby…yes that feels so good."

He moans as he eats her pussy and ass. She is now dripping wet and he is as hard as he's going to get. He stands up, unhooks her bra as it drops to the floor, grabs her tits and squeezes them. He kisses her neck from behind, she turns to face him, and they kiss passionately, their tongues playing with each other. He sucks on her lower lip and pulls on it gently. She sucks on his tongue. He squeezes her tits and rubs her nipples with his thumbs and index fingers. "Oh this is so heavenly," they both realize. He rubs his hard cockhead over and in between her pussy lips and the warmth of her pussy juices is enough to make him shoot his big warm load of cum but he doesn't dare do that yet.

He shoves his big thick long hard cock inside her wet warm juicy dripping wet pussy, balls deep and she moans loud. He starts to pump his cock harder, faster and deeper inside her. Her ass slaps against his pelvis and upper thighs as he pounds her wet warm pussy hard and deep. She pushes her ass out even more so he can really grab it with both his hands, squeeze it, spread it open and really fuck her pussy like it needs a beating. Her pussy juices dripping all over his hard cock and balls. He pulls out his cock and tells her to suck it.

She turns around to face him, kneels down and starts to suck his hard cock, tasting her own pussy on it. She moans as she grabs his ass with both her hands and pulls it towards her so she can really deepthroat his cock. Her throat is making delicious wet sounds of getting fucked by a big hard cock. Her saliva drips from around her mouth as she sucks his hard cock. She then puts his juicy balls in her mouth and sucks on them, licking them all around.

He can't wait to fuck her pussy so he lifts her up and she wraps her legs around his waist. He grabs her ass while she wraps her arms around his neck and shoulders and fucks her pussy deep. She moans with excitement. He kisses her neck and sucks on it as he fucks her standing up.

All this while, no one has walked in the restroom but right at that moment, they hear the bathroom door open. They both look at each other and suddenly stop moving. His hard cock still inside her pussy, they both pause for what seems like twenty seconds. They hear the tap shut off, the bathroom door closes, they giggle and he starts pounding her pussy again. He then helps her off, shuts the toilet cover close, sits on it and she sits on his cock to ride it like a cowgirl. He grabs her bare ass and helps her ride his big hard throbbing cock up and down, up and down, up and down. Her pussy juices dripping all over his cock and balls, making them wet and shiny. He buries his face in her tits and sucks on her nipples with one hand squeezing her tits, while the other holding her ass cheek. He is about to cum and so is she.

She starts to squeeze her pussy and ass over his cock as she orgasms. "Oh God Sam I'm cumming."

"Oh baby yes cum for me…cum on my hard cock baby," he says.

She starts to moan louder and cums on his hard cock. They kiss wildly as she cums.

He can't take it anymore. Hearing her cum is making

him cum. "I'm gonna cum baby."

They both look at each other and she nods with approval that he can cum inside her. At that very instance, he moans out: "Aaahhhhh fuck!"

She covers his mouth because he is kind of loud. His moans are muffled as he cums his big load of cum inside her wet, warm juicy pussy. He shakes rhythmically as he cums every last drop of his cum inside her, filling her pussy up with his hot man juice.

15 YACHT ZADDY

"It's a MATCH!" appears on the phone screen. Nina has a smile on her face. It is very gratifying for her to see that image on the screen. It is the equivalent of hitting a jackpot on a slot machine for her or matching symbols on a scratch card. She just swiped right on a picture of a handsome older man and was hoping it would be a match. His profile was carefully created with curated pictures of him showing off his opulent and active lifestyle. She is as equally impressed with his pictures as she is with his ability to use just the right bait in his profile to catch plenty of fish. "He has to be a player," she thinks.

One of the pictures is with him on a yacht, shirtless and wearing a pair of white shorts. You can see his strong muscular body even at his age of 48. They do say men are like wine – they get better with age. He is holding the wheel of the yacht with one hand and has a beer in the other hand. He is looking straight ahead. She wonders who took that shot of him and gets a little jealous envisioning one of his whores with him on his yacht.

One of the other pictures is in what seems to be a study in a beautiful big mansion with him sitting behind a big antique-looking desk made from seemingly expensive wood. The walls are covered with interesting paintings, stuffed heads of exotic animals and lots of antique-looking swords and guns. On the desk is a Cuban cigar box, a globe made out of marble it seems, a pile of old leather-bound books with golden inscription, and a bunch of other interesting looking objects which she has no idea of. But the sexiest part of the picture is him. He is wearing a dark blue suit with a burgundy silk handkerchief in the front suit pocket and his hands are in front of him resting on top of a world map. He is wearing some expensive watch and a couple of big rings on his fingers. He's got slightly greying temples, a- three-day stubble on his strong chiseled jawline and he is looking directly into the camera lens with his dreamy eyes saying, "I have you! Let me take you on an adventure of your lifetime."

He definitely has Nina. That picture just made her a little wet. She starts to daydream about getting fucked by him on his yacht in the middle of the Caribbean Sea or on the Greek shoreline with the white-washed houses of Santorini in the background and cloudless blue skies above.

"Oh you can fuck me any way you want, anywhere you want Gabriel," she mumbles after reading his name on his profile. "What a powerful name too…"

She has to force herself out of the daydream before she starts masturbating in her kitchen while eating her lucky charms. She sighs loudly and starts to go about her day. She doesn't want to send him a message just yet, since on Bumble the women have to send the first message. She wants to leave him wondering for a little bit. She has 24 hours to message first so she has plenty of time to decide on her greeting. For now, she has to do her Sunday chores.

She goes about doing her laundry while wearing her underwear – the joys of living alone. She has her Sunday-morning-chores Spotify playlist playing in the background. As she does her chores, she can't get Gabriel out of her mind. She wonders what he does for a living, whether he is a businessman or just born into wealth. Does he have a girlfriend or girlfriends? A wife? Fuck buddies? Does he have or want kids? Is he faithful? How big is his dick? Does he like to have his ass eaten? So many unanswered questions...

After having done all her laundry, she decides to shave her whole body because she never knows how her Sundays turn out. Sex can never be ruled out and she wants to be prepared. Sundays are the busiest days for dating apps and she's already talking to a bunch of guys but none of them have caught her attention and intrigue as Gabriel has.

She makes herself a bath and gets in with her phone right by her side on the edge of the tub. She opens up her Bumble app and flips through his pictures again. She is tempted to rub her pussy while looking at his pictures and resists just for a minute. She gives in to the temptation and starts rubbing her clit and pussy lips under water. The smell of her scented vanilla candle burning on the sink, her fruity bubble bath fragrance, the hot bath water and pictures of Gabriel are just the right setting for her imagination to run wild and make her pussy throb with ecstasy. She looks at his pictures and rubs her pussy and clit and feels an orgasm building up. She starts rubbing more vigorously as her orgasm nears and her humming moans turn into screaming moans. Her body quivers and convulses as she has the most explosive self-pleasured orgasm she has had in a while. She then rests her head back on the edge of the tub and dozes off for a bit.

She is woken up by a phone call. It is her best friend Ariana so she picks up. "Hey bitch. What's up?" she answers.

"Nothing hoe...what are you doing?" Ariana asks.

"Oh nothing...just in the bath trying to decide what to write to this hot ass daddy I have matched with on Bumble today."

"Ooo screenshot bitch! Send...send!"

Nina screenshots Gabriel's profile photos and sends

them to Ariana.

"Oh shit girl! He's a fuckin' zaddy!" Ariana exclaims.

"Right? He's rich as fuck too. Look at him flexin' on that badass yacht and those paintings, guns and animal heads on his wall. I want him to tie me up, blindfold me, gag me and fuck me raw girl!" Nina replies.

"You and me both bitch."

"But me first!"

They both laugh out loud.

"So girl, Michelle, Jocelyn and I were going to brunch…wanna come with?" Ariana asks.

"Let me message this beefcake first girl and see if he wants to fuck cuz I can brunch with you any day but I don't wanna miss out on this five course meal, ya hear me?" Nina says.

"Loud and clear bitch! Do your thang. Hit me up later."

"I will." Nina gets out of the bath and dries up.

She decides to send him a quick message because the more she thinks about what to write to him, the more confused she gets. "Hi Gabriel…I'm not on this app much so I'd much rather talk to you on the phone. Here's my number: 909-713-4130" she writes and starts getting dressed for the day.

As she sits on her couch and watches Netflix, her phone rings. The number isn't saved in her contacts so she knows it's either a telemarketer or Gabriel. She picks up and to her surprise it is Gabriel. That was quick. It is a short phone call as he is ready to meet her and sets up a time and place for them to have lunch. It is one of the fanciest sushi bars in town. She gets super excited and nervous as she starts getting dressed for her date with him.

She orders an Uber when she's ready to go and arrives at the fancy restaurant right on time. She sees him already sitting at a reserved table. He sees her too and waves at her. He stands up as she approaches him. His eyes do a quick top-to-bottom and they light up. Nina is dressed to kill in her short red dress and black red-bottom stilettos. They kiss each other on the cheek and he pulls her chair for her and helps her get seated.

"I'm so glad you called so promptly. I hate the back and forth messaging on dating apps and then fizzling out," she says.

"Yes me too. I'd much rather talk on the phone and set a date. Why waste time right?" he says.

"Agreed"

"So what do you do Nina? I love that name by the way."

"Oh wow thank you!" she blushes. "I'm a Social Media Manager at a PR company in downtown."

"That's nice. Sounds like fun."

"It truly is. I love my job. What do you do? You seem to have such a fancy lifestyle."

"Haha…yes I do indeed. I'm in the family ship-building business."

"What? Wow…haha…I have never even heard of that before. So what does that mean exactly? Your company builds cruise ships or something?"

"Something like that."

"That is so cool."

"Enough small talk…lets order food cuz I'm starving!"

"I'm with you on that."

They order food and flirt with each other the whole time. The food arrives and they gobble it up pretty quick. The wine with the sushi is making them even more flirtatious.

"So I have my yacht anchored right here in the marina. Do you want to check it out?" he asks.

"Fuck yeah I do. I've only been on a yacht once in my life," she replies.

"Alright then…lets go Nina." He pays for the check with two $100 bills and doesn't even bother getting change back. They both walk out and he hands his valet parking ticket to the attendant.

A matt black Lamborghini pulls up a few minutes later.

"Holy shit that's a nice car!" she exclaims.

"Haha…thanks. Wait till you see my yacht," he says.

He ushers her into the passenger seat of his lambo and closes the wing door for her. He sits in and presses on the gas to impress her with the speed of the car. The faster the car goes, the wetter her pussy gets. It's almost like the speedometer needle is indicating the scale of her wetness.

They arrive at the marina and he escorts her to the most stylish and expensive looking yacht of the bunch. He holds her hand and guides her onto the anchored yacht's deck.

"Oh my fuckin' God! Are you serious? This shit is insane!" she exclaims with a big grin on her face.

He laughs. "Let me give you a quick tour." He shows her around the yacht and all she can think of is when he will make her daydream come true and fuck the shit out of her in all the sexy corners of this beauty.

They come to the master bedroom of the yacht. It's furnished with a King-sized bed that looks freshly made with fluffed-up pillows. The whole room has shiny lacquered wood furniture with a big screen TV, bedside tables, wine cabinets, wooden floors, drawers for days. It looks straight out of a magazine.

She dives onto the bed on her back. "I've found my favorite spot."

"Oh be my guest. Let me grab some champagne," he says.

She snoops around a little while he is gone. She opens one of the many drawers in the room and discovers some serious BDSM toys. "Holy shit Gabriel. You're a kinky bastard," she whispers. "Damn boy!"

He comes back with his shirt unbuttoned with two champagne glasses in one hand and a bottle of Dom Perignon in the other. He finds her holding up one of the nipple clamps. "I see you have found my toys." He pours a glass for her and hands it to her.

"Uh…yeah! Do you plan on torturing me with this shit?" she says.

"On the contrary, the toys are designed to give pleasure. Have you never tried BDSM before?"

"I've had rough sex but never been with a guy with such an extensive collection of bondage toys."

"Well you never know. Once you try it, you might actually never want to have sex any other way."

"Hmm…interesting"

"You have to trust me that I won't do anything to hurt you."

"I don't even know you Gabriel."

"If I wanted to hurt you, I would've done it already Nina."

"Well I do know there is a thin line between pleasure and pain. I've always wanted to try this stuff."

"Then let me have the privilege of introducing you to the world of BDSM."

"Don't I need a safe word to let you know if I want you to stop doing whatever the hell you're doing to me?"

"Sure. You decide what it will be."

"Umm…how about 'stop'?"

"Hahaha…That's fine. And if something is obstructing your mouth and you cannot speak, just tap anywhere twice and I'll stop."

"And what if I can't tap with my hands or speak?"

"Then just groan."

"Oh Jesus! I'm in trouble!"

"Drink up that glass cuz you need to be buzzed for lesson 1."

She gulps the champagne down quickly, almost eager to start.

He takes the glass from her and sets it aside. "Stand up," he commands.

She obeys.

He places his hand on her back and pulls her towards him. They look into each other's eyes and before he can lean in to kiss her, she grabs his shirt and kisses him. They kiss passionately and start undressing each other with haste.

She touches his chest and kisses his neck. He grabs both her ass cheeks with both his hands and squeezes them hard. She bites his neck. He holds her by her waist and turns her around and pushes her on the bed. She rests the side of her face on the bed and sticks her ass up in the air. He grabs both her wrists and grabs a piece of rope from his toy drawer. He ties her hands behind her back.

"Oh shit. And it begins…" she says.

He slaps her ass hard, gets down on his knees, spits on her butt hole and licks it. He then grabs a butt plug from his drawer and puts it in her mouth. She sucks on it. He then spits on her ass hole again and slowly inserts the butt plug in her ass. "Does that feel ok?" he asks.

"Yes it's fine. I like anal," she responds.

He pushes the butt plug all the way in and she gasps for air. He rubs her already wet pussy and then spreads her ass cheeks so her pink pussy lips spread open. He sticks his warm wet soft tongue inside her pussy and then slides it up and down between her wet pussy lips. She moans with pleasure. He licks her clit with the tip of his tongue. She moans louder. She is now dripping wet. He helps her up so she is sitting on her knees facing him. He grabs the nipple clamps from the drawer.

"Are you ready for this?" he asks her.

"You can do whatever you want Gabriel. I'm loving every bit of this so far."

He takes the nipple clamps and places one of them on her erect nipples. He looks at her face to see how she feels. She looks straight back and smiles. He is impressed by her pain tolerance. He places the other one on her other nipple. He then takes his hard erect cock and puts it in her mouth. She starts sucking his dick like she has been starving for it. She deepthroats his cock until she gags on it.

"Yeah! Just like that baby! Choke on this big dick baby!" he shouts.

She spits on his dick and he grabs her head and fucks her throat deep and holds his dick in for a few seconds. Her face starts to turn red and she groans. He pulls his cock out and slaps her face with it. He rubs his hard cock, which is now covered with her saliva, all over her face. She licks and sucks his balls.

He grabs a longer piece of rope and ties her feet together by the ankles. She is completely helpless and at his mercy now. He then grabs a ball gag and straps it on her head. He then picks out a black blindfold and ties it over her eyes.

She has never felt so powerless and aroused before. It is the ultimate position of submission for her.

He grabs her and turns her around so she has her face down on the bed and her ass up in the air. He then spreads her ass cheeks and shoves his big hard thick cock in her wet warm juicy pussy and starts to fuck her balls deep.

She immediately starts moaning. It is a very strange sensation for her not being able to move her arms and legs, not being able to speak or see. The only other usable sense is her hearing. And the sound of his body slapping against hers fills the room as he slaps her ass hard while pounding her pussy hard, fast and deep with every stroke.

Her pussy is dripping wet and creaming all over his cock shaft. He watches his hard cock being swallowed by her pussy lips with her pussy juices making his dick drenched. Her moans start to get louder and more intense and he senses her about to cum. He starts pounding her pussy harder and faster and she starts to shake as she cums all over his hard cock while moaning loud.

He pulls off her ball gag and shoves his big hard cock in her mouth. He pumps his hard dick in and out balls deep into her throat making her gag on his big dick. He then puts his balls in her mouth and she sucks and licks them eagerly. He is about to cum as well so he starts stroking his dick while she sucks and licks his big balls.

He starts moaning louder. "Fuck baby I'm gonna cum…I'm gonna cum. Aaaaaaahhhh! Fuck! Open your mouth. Aaahhhhhh fuck! Yeah baby! Take this big load of cum. Swallow it!" He cums all over her face with her tongue sticking out. She catches some in her mouth while the rest of it covers her face. She sucks the last drops of his cum out of his cock head and giggles.

"That was fuckin' awesome!" she shouts.

"I'm glad you liked round 1," he says. "The bathroom is right there if you want to freshen up."

"Umm…a little help here please?"

He laughs and takes off all the bondage gear she has on.

They both freshen up and lie back in bed. They're exhausted and end up dozing off.

Forty minutes into their afternoon nap on a yacht, his phone rings and wakes them up.

"Hey man. What's up?" he answers. "Oh I'm in the middle of something right now…why…I'm with someone right now at the yacht…yes it's a girl…I don't know actually…let me ask her and I'll text you back…ok bye."

"What was all that about?" she asks.

"That was my childhood buddy asking me if he could come over with a couple of our friends."

"Here? You mean right now?"

"Yes…and I wanted to ask you if that's ok."

"Well…I guess…but what is going to happen here? Do you want to gang bang me or something?" she laughs.

"Well do you want to be gangbanged?"

"Umm…I don't know. I've already had a first time BDSM session with you. I don't know what else I can take."

"Ok listen…tell you what…how about you meet my friends and see how you like them. And if you guys get along, maybe it could turn into a little gangbang."

"You say that like you do this kinda thing all the time

Gabriel."

"To be honest...I've only done it once before and it was in my college days."

"Hmm really...well fuck it. YOLO right?"

"That's right! That's the spirit baby," he leans over and kisses her.

Twenty minutes later, Gabriel's friends arrive. Nina thought it was going to be maybe two more guys but they're actually three more guys. She gets nervous thinking about getting gangbanged by four guys. She's in the sexually liberal spirit right now and is up for the challenge.

Introductions and greetings are made and everyone takes a seat at the deck. Champagne is poured into glasses, there is laughter, there is flirting, everyone is in swimming attire. Everyone is getting tipsier. One of the guys rolls up a joint and it's being passed around. Everyone at this point is high, pretty buzzed and feeling pretty great.

"What do you say guys? Should we take this party inside?" Gabriel asks everyone.

Everyone agrees. Gabriel holds Nina's hand and escorts her into the bedroom. The three friends follow eagerly.

Nina gets on the bed and takes off her clothes. "Come on boys. I'm all yours. Fuck me like the whore that I am."

All the men get naked lightning fast and gather around her with their dicks in their hands, spitting on their palms and stroking their hard cocks.

Gabriel just sits on a chair and watches.

"Aren't you gonna join baby?" Nina asks him.

"Right now I just wanna watch you getting fucked baby," he responds.

One of the guys takes his hard dick and puts it in her mouth. Another guy spreads her legs open and starts eating her pussy while the third guy is rubbing, squeezing and sucking on her tits. She starts moaning and the guys are feasting on her body like wild sex beasts.

The guy who was eating her pussy lifts her by the waist,

lies on his back and places her on top of his hard erect cock. She starts riding his dick, while she sucks another guy's dick and strokes another one. She starts really getting into this cock buffet. Her inner porn star begins to come out. She rides his dick like a wild cowgirl while getting facefucked by one of the guys.

"Fuck her ass. She likes that," Gabriel says while smoking a cigar in the corner and sipping on a glass of scotch while watching the live action porn on his yacht.

One of the guys gets behind her and she leans down while he puts his hard cock in her ass. She is now being double-penetrated by Gabriel's friends. One guy stands in front of her face so she can suck him while being fucked in her ass and pussy. All her available holes are filled with dicks. Her pussy and ass are being rammed with dicks and she has never felt so sexually fulfilled. She starts to moan louder as she reaches orgasm. Her whole body shakes and she cums as her ass and pussy is ravaged by dicks.

The guys take turns fucking her ass, pussy and mouth…making sure all the three guys get to fuck all her three holes. Gabriel watches the action and starts to stroke his own cock. Everyone is moaning and groaning.

Nina is sweating from head to toe; her face is covered with her own spit and sweat. She never thought a gangbang could be this much fun. If it wasn't for Gabriel's persuasiveness, she might never have tried this in all her life. She is fucked in every position possible by these guys. There is a dick in her pussy, ass and mouth at all times.

The guys all start moaning louder and start fucking faster. She can sense they are all pretty much about to cum. They all pull out their dicks from her holes and she gets down on her knees. Gabriel joins his naked friends standing around Kneeling Nina.

She is sucking everyone's dick by turn and stroking the other dicks with both her hands. She is going to experience her first bukkake ever. She looks into the men's eyes and the look of ecstasy on their faces is turning her on even more. The first guy starts to moan louder than everyone else and is about to cum. He shoots his big load of cum all over her open mouth and face. She starts to rub her clit now as the second guy strokes his dick over her face while she licks and sucks his balls. He shoots his big thick load of warm cum all over her face and tits. Then cums the third guy all over her eyes and forehead. She wipes off the cum from her eyes so she can see.

It is Gabriel's turn now. His towering Adonis body stands at her knees while she looks up into his ecstasy-filled eyes. She rubs her clit vigorously as he strokes his dick faster. She sucks his balls while looking up into his eyes. He moans louder and louder and his body starts to shake. Watching him in pleasure makes her reach orgasm as well. He starts cumming on her face and she starts cumming simultaneously. He shoots his big warm thick load of cum in her mouth. He wants her to swallow all his cum. With her cum-drenched face, she sucks his dick head and takes every last drop of his cum and gulps it down.

FIND ME ON FACEBOOK

www.facebook.com/readerotica

www.ingramcontent.com/pod-product-compliance
Lightning Source LLC
Chambersburg PA
CBHW030753110726
47900CB00008B/2583